D1707147

DEAD MAN CAKEWALKING

APPLE ORCHARD COZY MYSTERIES BOOK 20

CHELSEA THOMAS

Big + LITTLE PRESS

Copyright & Disclaimer

Dead Man Cakewaling © Chelsea Thomas, 2023

Disclaimer -- All rights reserved. No part of this eBook may be reproduced, stored or transmitted in any form, or by any means, including mechanical or electronic, without written permission from the author.

While the author has made every effort to ensure that the ideas, guidelines and information printed in this eBook are safe, they should be used at the reader's discretion. The author cannot be held responsible for any personal or commercial damage arising from the application or misinterpretation of information presented herein.

This book is a work of fiction. Names, characters, places and incidents are the products of the author's imagination or used fictitiously. Any resemblance to the actual events, locales or persons, living or dead, is entirely coincidental.

Join the Chelsea Thomas Reader Club

Cover Design: Priscilla Pantin

 Created with Vellum

1

THE WEDDING PLANNER

*I*n the picturesque town of Pine Grove, where snowy hillsides were home to playing children, and every person on Main Street sipped hot cocoa from steaming cups, an almost year break from murder had residents tittering with excitement.

As we headed toward reindeer and gingerbread houses and presents under the tree, folks almost seemed to forget that killers were about as common as apple pie in our quaint small town.

It was almost as if they didn't expect the tragedy that would soon befall them.

As a bride-to-be, I was thinking about anything *but* murder that holiday season. For some reason, my fiancé and I had decided to get married on Christmas day, and the whole ordeal had been complicated, to say the least.

My wedding planner, for instance, had been far more interested in my life story than in planning my wedding. The woman's name was Kayla Bella, and she insisted on running through all the major details every time I saw her, including on our final walk through of the event barn at my family apple orchard before my impending nuptials.

"Chelsea Thomas, world-famous sleuth and Pine Grove's hardest working orphan!" She breezed into the kitchen, stopping only to air-kiss me on one cheek, then the other. "Wedding planning is so much more fun when your client is a local legend. Tell me again about how your parents died, then you moved here, then you transformed from emotional wreck to self-assured sleuth overnight!"

Kayla had veneers that looked as though they'd been pried from the mouth of a local weather girl. Her white cable-knit sweater pooled onto dark-wash jeans, and she spoke with a bubbly staccato that was blasphemous to all us non-morning people.

In her re-telling of my major life events, Kayla had skipped the part where I'd gotten left at the altar. She hadn't mentioned how that evil ex had recently moved to my small-town, either. But she'd gotten the major plot points of my life right enough, which made me wonder just how much the people of Pine Grove had been gossiping about me.

I grumbled some version of hello as Kayla handed me a coffee.

"Just a few days 'til the big one! You ready?"

She could have been talking about murder or marriage, though how could she have known a new victim would turn up soon?

Kayla had a habit of talking before I had a chance to answer her questions. To be honest, I kind of liked it. "Oh! How does Detective Hudson look in his tux?" she said. "I bet be looks so hot, if you don't mind me saying. Nothing better than a cop in a penguin suit, am I right? I know I'm right."

Blood rushed to my face. I reached for a response but came up with nothing more than a mouthful of air.

"Listen, before we get into the wedding planning thing, I heard this story about a mystery you solved at some coroner's house. You have to tell me about that one!"

"You're not here to gossip, Kayla. You're here to work." My aunt, Miss May, stomped into the kitchen, pulling on her favorite jean jacket. "C'mon. Let's go check out the event barn."

Kayla shot a look at me as she followed Miss May out. It was as if she thought the two of us were schoolgirls conspiring against Miss May to gab later. I didn't know what kind of face to make back. I bared my teeth, kind of like I was smiling, and I made my eyes go big and wide. Kayla looked frightened as she hurried out.

Mission accomplished?

Kayla kept runnin' her mouth as we headed out toward the event barn. "You are just so impressive, Chelsea. I mean, you've barely been here over a year and you've already met a man, gotten engaged, and become co-owner of the family business!"

The truth was I'd been living back at Miss May's for well over a year by that point. And I'd only been named co-owner of the family business, *The Thomas Fruit and Fir Farm*, thanks to her generosity. But as I looked out over the farm's rolling hills, a satisfied warmth filled my belly. It was Christmas tree season, so the farm had been crawling with Christmas-tree shoppers for weeks. That meant our little business had helped bring extra holiday cheer to so many homes that year, and I couldn't deny the satisfaction in that fact.

We entered the event barn to find Teeny already inside, adjusting the tea-lights on one of a dozen huge, circular tables. Teeny was a bottle-blonde bottle rocket, and she was the only person on earth who could have trumped Kayla Bell's energy that morning.

"Finally, you're here!" Teeny bustled over to me and wrapped me up in a big hug. I could smell the same perfume she'd been wearing since I was a little girl. A smile crossed my face as I breathed it in. "I was beginning to think the wedding had been called off. Oh boy. Sorry. Your last wedding was called off. I shouldn't say stuff like that. It could trigger memories of getting left at the altar."

"Stop talking, Teeny," said Miss May. "You're making it worse."

Teeny covered her mouth so only her big blue eyes were showing.

"Great to see you, Teeny," said Kayla, laughing. "Hey, before we get started, were you at the coroner's house that time Chelsea solved the mystery there? Miss May won't let her talk about it."

"That's because you're here to work, lady!" Teeny said.

Kayla groaned. "Fine." She whipped out a clipboard and a pen, fastening a much more serious look to her face. "Let's go through last minute details and we'll run through the day, make sure nobody has any questions that need answered."

Kayla's shift to business-mode pleased both Teeny and Miss May, and the three of them fell into the familiar rat-a-tat of wedding planning. I, however, couldn't focus on the details of my wedding. The way I saw it, the ball was in motion, and it was time to let it all play out.

Besides, I had a feeling a murder was coming, and I knew better than to plan in the face of chaos.

2

PRICKLY PINES

*H*ere's an abridged version of the story of my relationship with my ex-boyfriend, Michael Gherkin.

We met on an app. His main photo was a picture of him wearing a nice suit and smoking a cigar. That should have been my first warning.

Our first date was at *Tavern on the Green*, a five-star restaurant in New York's Central Park. I was young (ish). The splashy location impressed me. Mike did not. I agreed to a second date, and this is something for which I have no excuse.

After six months, Mike had assumed the role of C.O.O. of my interior design business. I still can't tell you what those letters stood for. But he handled all the financial stuff, which I liked.

On our wedding day, Mike left me standing at the altar like a bag of forgotten groceries. That night, I threw my wedding dress in a dumpster. Also that night, I learned that he'd shut me out of the business, and claimed all the accounts, and there was nothing I could do about it.

Fast forward a few years. Mike is engaged to a new woman, Priscilla. Curly-headed and gorgeous in every way I'm not. *Fun, right?* The two of them move to <u>my</u> small town. I decide to take the high road, which is the road labelled "Be Nice to Mike".

Fast forward a bit more, and the two of them are strolling through the evergreens at my family farm — just hours after Kayla Bell headed home — shopping for the perfect Christmas tree to place in the perfect window in their perfect new home.

Gross.

After I spotted them, I took a deep breath, and approached with a smile. "If I remember correctly, you're a Douglas Fir fan?"

Mike grinned. "Remember that eight-footer we got when we were living in that little place in SoHo? It was way too big."

Priscilla clung to Mike's arm amiably, seemingly unthreatened by me, the ex-girlfriend who had popped out of the pines. The woman had never seemed threatened by me, in fact. *Am I not threatening at all?* I thought. *Maybe I need to whiten my teeth or something.*

"This year we're looking for a white spruce." She smiled. Her teeth were whiter than snow, of course. And her eyes were bluer than God's favorite ocean. I liked her despite these obvious flaws. "White spruces have those stiff little needles. They don't fall off as much, right?"

"You know your trees, Priscilla." I shot a quick glance over to Mike. *What was it with this guy and falling for women who have a strong knowledge of all things coniferous?*

They both laughed. Priscilla replied before Mike had the chance. "My parents were sticklers for white spruce. That little needle fact is the only one I have."

"It's correct," I said, beginning to lead them toward our grove of white spruce trees. "White spruces hang on to their needles better, and the wood is strong, so the branches support ornaments well."

"We don't have any ornaments." The conversation had been so friendly to that point, but Mike's gruff tone turned us in a new direction...

"Because we're building a meaningful collection of our own." Priscilla spoke in a way that gave me the impression they'd had this conversation before. "What do you think, Chelsea? I want to buy ornaments on our travels, find pieces that are meaningful to us. The tree might be spare for the first few years of our marriage, but one day it will be filled with precious memories. Mike wants to buy a bunch of red and gold balls from the dollar store and call it a day."

My eyes widened. I did not want to be in the middle of an argument between Mike and his new fiancée. Chelsea Babble built up in my throat like a volcano about to erupt. I knew before I spoke that I was powerless to stop it. "White spruce is my favorite of the spruces," I said, swallowing hard. "Blue spruce is good too though. You really can't go wrong with a spruce. I want to make a joke about 'sprucing' something up, but I can't figure out a good punchline. So have you two set a date for your wedding yet?"

"Announced it yesterday," said Mike, voice turning angry as he continued. "It's just ridiculous to have a naked tree. We can't have anyone over if we don't decorate it. It's pathetic and it's morally wrong."

Did I leave Mike's irrational anger and crazed morality out of the story of our relationship? Weird. Yeah. The guy was intense in every single way. Sometimes that was a good thing. But when I'd been with him, his strong opinions and uncompromising moral superiority was a constant source of conflict.

Ironic, considering he left me at the altar and absconded with my business. But that's what these 'moral high ground' people are like sometimes. They use a public display of morals to cover up the fact that they're corrupt narcissists.

But let's get back to Priscilla and Mike. He was red in the face, and her nostrils were so wide you could have shoved a hula hoop through them.

"It is not pathetic to want to build a meaningful collection of ornaments," she said.

"I don't want my Christmas tree to display every little detail about my private life. That's kitschy. Trees should be simple and elegant. Chelsea agrees with me. I know it. That was how she used to approach her interior design."

"Don't bring Chelsea into this," said Priscilla. "You left the poor girl at the altar."

I didn't love being talked about like I wasn't there. Also, I think it would have been more fitting to describe Priscilla as 'the poor girl,' considering she was the one who was going to end up marrying Mike (barring a repeat performance at the altar). But I really, really did not want to get caught up in the drama, so I pointed at the tallest tree in sight and said, "That one is humongous! We've been growing it since I was nine!"

After a few minutes, the bickering couple cooled down. Well, Mike just stopped talking, and Priscilla avoided eye contact with him as she moved from one White Spruce to the next with a discerning eye. It was awkward, partially because I feared I might have been glowing from the warm light of satisfaction building within me.

Marrying Mike would have been murder. And that's a fate I wouldn't wish on my worst enemy...

3

HOLIDAY HORRORS

J stepped into the warm embrace of *Grandma's* with a small smile, and a sense of ease washed over me. The place was packed with diners, and the pleasant din of chatter and laughter filled the air. Teeny bustled from table to table, making sure her customers were happy. A little girl sipped hot cocoa, whipped cream all over her nose. Miss May waved me over from our VIP booth in back.

Teeny arrived at the table two steps ahead of me. "Ha! Beat ya!"

"I wasn't aware we were racing," I said.

"That's probably why I won." She settled into the booth beside Miss May as I took the seat across the table. "My restaurant is so majestic around the holidays, don't you think?"

"It's wonderful, Teeny," Miss May looked at me when she spoke, so I could tell she was humoring Teeny.

"Don't play Kate with me," said Teeny. "I'm old enough to know that look."

"Do you mean placate?" I asked.

"No. I mean 'play Kate'. It's when you want someone to stop talking so you tell them what they want to hear. It all started with a girl named Kate a hundred years ago, and it took off from there."

I opened my mouth to explain the wrongness of the 'Teenyism,' then thought better of it. "Did you hear about what happened with Mike and Priscilla at the farm today?"

"I told her," said Miss May, sipping her coffee. "She was disgusted."

"Disgusted but not shocked," said Teeny. "The guy was a regular Joe Jerk when you were dating him. I never said anything because I don't interfere in other people's lives. But the whole time you were dating I wanted to shake you and say 'Drop this guy to the curb, Chelsea!'"

"Maybe next time don't keep that to yourself," I said. "You know I'm getting married on Christmas, right?"

"And you know I love Detective McBeefy," said Teeny. "Wayne is the freshest catch in Pine Grove, by a long shot."

"From what Chelsea told me, I thought it sounded like she did a great job handling the conflict between Mike and Priscilla," said Miss May. "Handled it just how she would have handled it with any other customer."

"Yeah." I scoffed at my own expense. "Lots of babbling and a general fear of conflict kept me from getting too wrapped up in it. But I came away appreciating Wayne even more than I already did. He would never describe someone's perspective on Christmas tree décor as 'pathetic' or 'morally wrong.'"

"If I'd have known how much of a jerk Mike was, I never would have given him the table by the window in the back room," said Teeny.

"Hold on." I narrowed my eyes. "Mike is here right now?"

"He and Priscilla each ordered my Santa's Special Squash. Sat down about half an hour ago."

"How did they seem?" said Miss May.

"Hungry. And like they'd been arguing about Christmas trees all day."

Miss May sighed. "How about we change the subject? Tell us more about this Santa's Squash dish you're making."

"I'd love to!" Teeny clasped her hands together. "Santa's Special Squash is a masterpiece of flavors and textures. This dish features roasted acorn squash halves, filled to the brim with a medley of seasonal veggies, including sautéed Brussels sprouts, caramelized onions, and earthy wild mushrooms. Topped with a sprinkle of toasted pecans and a drizzle of tangy balsamic glaze, this colorful creation is a delight to vegetarians and meat-eaters alike!"

I tossed my head back and laughed. "Wow. You just described that dish like it was a prize on *The Price Is Right*. Sounds delicious."

"I'm trying to vary up my offerings this holiday season. Everybody has Gingerbread House Pancakes, and Christmas Cookie Cake, and Rudolph's Red-nosed Risotto, you know?"

"Literally no one else serves those dishes," I said. "What?"

"Thank you for saying that," said Teeny. "But still. I thought I needed Santa's Squash to keep things fresh."

"You don't need to thank me, I'm just telling the truth," I said.

"I really appreciate that," said Teeny. "You're sweet."

"But I'm actually, literally –"

"Shh!" Miss May held up her hand and I stopped talking. Voices rose in an argument from the back room.

My heart skipped as I recognized the familiar timbre of

Mike's voice, raised in anger and frustration. Memories flooded my mind, reminding me of a time when our futures seemed intertwined. But that was before everything changed for the better. Before Detective McBeefy swept me off my feet.

Priscilla's voice intermingled with Mike's. It was a volatile duet, their voices crashing against one another like waves on a rocky shoreline. I strained to catch snippets of the heated exchange but couldn't make out more than the occasional insult or defiant yelp.

Emotions swirled through my body. Were they remnants of love? Were they the feelings of lingering hurt? Or were they pure, morbid curiosity?

Suddenly, Mike and Priscilla stumbled out of the back room. Much to my surprise, they were laughing, and in the middle of what appeared to be a wild game of keep away. Mike held a bouquet of roses above his head and Priscilla jumped up for them.

"Give them back, you bully!" she said.

"Not until you tell me how handsome I am!"

Even I can admit, the scene was cute. In that moment, I saw a side of Mike I'd almost forgotten existed. Playful, invigorating, always ready to tease the people he loved. Seconds later, they'd stumbled back into the back room, continuing their game of keep away.

I helped Teeny close the restaurant that night. She was way, way, way (overly) thankful. But I get a weird buzz from setting things right again (maybe that's part of my love for solving crimes), so cleaning up was no big deal at all.

As I made my way through the restaurant, tidying up the tables and dimming the lights, a glimmer caught my eye. I bent down to get a closer look, my fingers brushing against a forgotten object hidden beneath one of the tables. With a sense of intrigue, I retrieved the item and found myself holding a new leather wallet, embossed with the name of some fancy Italian leather company.

A surge of anticipation washed over me as I flipped the wallet open. I liked the idea that I would be the one to return this wallet to its owner. They were going to be so relieved it had been found. So thankful. So appreciative of my help.

As I gingerly opened the wallet, the supple leather parted to reveal a multitude of shiny credit cards, each branded with the name of a different bank. I flipped open the middle fold to reveal a driver's license.

My stomach plummeted as I saw the photo on the license. Mike's smug face was staring up at me. And the picture was annoyingly good.

In a flash, I saw myself running up credit card debt, buying new farm equipment for Miss May, and a leather jacket for Wayne, and a new wardrobe for myself. But deep down I knew I had to return the wallet. To do anything else would be morally wrong. You know, like preferring white spruce over Douglas fir.

4

MIKE DROPPED

My 60s Ford Thunderbird growled like a jungle cat as I cruised down Mike's street, keeping an eye out for his address.

"I still can't get over you in this car," said Miss May.

I smiled. "Me neither. I like it that way."

The people of Pine Grove had gifted me the car at the end of our last investigation. Every ride I'd taken since then had been positively joyous. The car — jet black, white interior, cherry-red rims — had more style than I ever could. While I sometimes missed my old blue pickup, riding around in my own personal Batmobile softened the bitter sting of nostalgia until it was barely more annoying than a bug bite.

"What house number did you say Mike was?" said Miss May.

"He's at 44 Maple." I scanned mailboxes as I drove. "There's 36... And 38... And 40..."

I slowed to a halt in front of the address on Mike's license. The brick house was the biggest on the block, with Corinthian columns propping up a decorative portico. The front door was an angry bright red and it had an iron knocker fastened to it like a balled-up fist.

The outline of the home had been traced in soft white Christmas lights. There was a stillness there that felt like it contained the entirety of the past and the whole, limitless future in a single moment. I waited before climbing out of the car, listening intently to the quiet all beautiful neighborhoods enjoy in those peaceful nights leading to Christmas. Looking back, I see I was grasping for something, or holding on to a world more perfect than the one I'd soon meet. But in that evening quiet, all I knew was that I'd found a wallet that I had to return.

The iron knocker was cold in my palm. I felt the significant weight of the thing as I pulled back to knock, so I let it come down slowly on the iron corollary on the door's front. One knock, then another and another, the sound of each evaporating as soon as it chimed, absorbed by the heavy wooden door.

"Maybe they're not home," said Miss May. "That's weird though. Those two went tree shopping, then they went out to dinner. How much more can one couple fit into a single day?"

"When Mike gets into 'party mode,' there's no telling how many chapters the night might have," I said. "Those times were kind of fun, actually."

"Let me knock." Miss May grabbed the knocker and brought it down with twice as much force as I'd used. I feared she'd crack the door in half, but it stayed strong. *Might be a lesson in there somewhere*, I thought. *Maybe... Don't be afraid to take charge? Or... People are stronger than you think?*

"Someone is definitely home," I said.

"Why do you think that?" said Miss May.

"For one thing, Mike's car is in the driveway. I know it's

his because it has all his stupid alma mater bumper stickers on it. We get it, you went to a good school."

"They could out somewhere in Priscilla's car though," said Miss May.

"Also, there's a light on over there." I gestured to a room at the far end of the house. "Mike was a huge stickler for electricity. He used to make it seem like I was purposefully murdering the environment every time I left the house without killing the lights. Then he got an app on his phone so he could make sure all the lights were off even after we'd gone out."

"And you were going to marry this person... why?"

"Young, naïve, abandonment issues from dead parents."

"Right," said Miss May. "Well, if they're home it would seem they don't want any guests. Should we leave the wallet in the mailbox or something?"

"Mike!" I knocked again. "We've got your wallet. You forgot it at *Grandma's*."

No answer.

"You OK, Chels?"

"Yeah. Just uh... You know that feeling you get before you find a dead body?"

"Unfortunately, yes."

I gave Miss May a tight smile. "I've got that feeling right now."

I made it inside Mike's house through an unlocked window around back. Seconds later, I'd let Miss May in through the back door, and we were padding through the home with careful steps.

"Mike? You in here? Priscilla?"

"The back door was open so we let ourselves in," said Miss May, shrugging at me. "We have your wallet."

As I crept through the house, two things distracted me:

1) I had an uneasy, tense feeling in my stomach that wouldn't go away.

2) I'm just going to say it: the interior design of the house was very, very bad. Everything was grey, beige, or white. The whole place made me feel like I was in the waiting room of my pediatrician's office in 1995. But we weren't there to criticize Mike's interior design choices, so I'm just going to leave it at that.

Blah!

Slowly, we made our way from a boring kitchen and down a long, ugly hallway, headed toward the softly lit room I'd noticed from outside. The ugly door to the room was closed, and an amber glow leaked out from under the door. I turned the budget, Home Depot doorknob. *OK. I'll stop. But it was SO ugly!*

The door opened to reveal a small den. The amber glow emanated from an old, worn-out lamp that cast flickering shadows across the room, painting the walls with a muted, sepia hue. The air felt heavy and hot, as if holding its breath, and a cheap pleather couch dressed the scene in a sharp, chemical smell.

My eyes darted around the room. A corner window was broken. Papers were scattered on the floor. A painting hung askew.

"Chelsea."

I turned. Miss May was squatting behind an antique writing desk — the nicest piece I'd seen in the house thus far.

"What is..." My voice trailed off. Mike was splayed out on the ground beside Miss May. A chill raced up my spine as I noticed blood pooled on the floor beside him.

I said Mike's name, but I did not expect a reply. The room suddenly felt like a twisted stage for a macabre play.

Kneeling beside Miss May, I reached out to touch Mike's shoulder, hoping for a sign of life, for some indication that this was all some terrible mistake, a practical joke played on me by an ex-boyfriend with whom I'd never shared a sense of humor.

But as my fingers made contact with his cold, lifeless flesh, a wave of despair washed over me. Mike was gone. A gasp escaped my lips, mingling with the stifled sob that threatened to consume me.

I stepped back, my mind racing with questions and disbelief. What had happened to Mike? Who had done this? And what secrets did this poorly decorated room hold that might reveal the truth behind this chilling discovery?

As I stood there, gazing at the lifeless form before me, I knew that this solemn moment marked an important change in my story. My time in Pine Grove had begun after Mike left me at the altar. Now Mike had left his life behind, and the only way I was going to feel better about any of it was to find his killer.

5

DEADLY NOTED

*I*t was surreal to see Mike lying there, so motionless, so devoid of life. During my time with him, he'd been anything but lifeless, often in a negative way.

My mind flashed back to a memory from the first year we were together. Mike's best friend had kept us waiting at a restaurant for over an hour. With each passing minute, Mike had gotten angrier and angrier, until finally he'd blown up at the waiter.

The memory flooded my mind. Suddenly, the gross décor of Mike's den fell away, and I was once again sitting in that restaurant, experiencing the night for the second time in the present moment.

"Hey!" Mike snapped his fingers at our waiter, an older woman with a frock of gray hair. "I ordered my wine half an hour ago. Where is it?"

The woman stammered. "I'm sorry. You told me you wanted to see the wine list, so I brought it. But you never ordered a glass."

"I ordered a glass of your California Syrah." Mike said it

like it was an irrefutable truth. I knew he was mistaken but wasn't sure how to set him straight without causing an even bigger scene. As I leaned forward, attempting to slide into the conversation, the waiter met Mike's scowl with a humble bow of the head.

"Must be my mistake," she said. "I'll be back with your Syrah shortly, and I'll be sure to take it off your bill."

Thankfully, the server was too far away to hear Mike mutter "you better take it off the bill." Still, once she was gone, I shrunk down in my seat so far, I thought I might fall onto the floor beneath the table.

My face, flushing hot and red with embarrassment and shame, brought me back to Mike's den, where he lay dead before me. I took a deep breath and blinked a few times, trying to orient myself.

"You OK, Chels?" said Miss May.

"Yeah." I shook myself out of my daze and glanced around the room, my gaze finally settling back on Mike's lifeless corpse. He'd been a bad boyfriend. Nonetheless, grief filled my body. For every time I'd seen Mike angry, there was another I'd seen him content. I suppose we're all multi-faceted. In that moment, the thought that Mike would never get to become the man I knew he could have been saddened me.

Words tumbled out of my mouth before my brain had a chance to register them. I talked about the first time I'd met Mike. I shared my memory of the time he was happiest (when he shot a hole in one and all his friends got jealous). A tear streaked down my face as I recalled the moment he'd proposed. I'd been so happy then, but I couldn't, for the life of me, tell you why.

Miss May interjected after a long pause. "That was really nice, how you just honored Mike's memory."

"We all deserve that, I think."

"Want to know an even better way to honor his memory?" I looked at her. She smirked and scrunched up her nose. "Let's catch his killer."

Just like that, we snapped into amateur detective mode. I kneeled to get a better look at Mike's body. He clutched car keys in his right hand, fingers clasped around the metal like he thought the keys could have kept him alive. The blood that had pooled on the floor originated at a large head-wound just above his forehead, but there did not appear to be any additional wounds on his body.

"You're not gonna like this, Chels."

I whipped my head around to find Miss May standing at a small, oak end table. She shook her head as I walked toward her, intently focused on a notepad resting on the table.

"What is it?" I asked.

Miss May stepped aside so I could get a closer look. There on the desk sat a simple letter, typed in a bold face font and printed on standard computer paper.

DEAR MIKE,

I CAN'T BELIEVE YOU'RE GETTING MARRIED AGAIN. YOU DON'T BELONG IN THIS TOWN. NOW YOU'RE GETTING WHAT YOU DESERVE.

- CHELSEA.

My hands went numb. An anxious warmth gripped my throat like the hands of a killer. "Somebody framed me for Mike's murder."

"Hello?" A female voice called out from somewhere inside the house. Keys clanged on a metal tray. "Mike?"

It was Priscilla. My eyes darted to the broken window, then to the door. There was no quick way out. We were trapped with my ex's dead body.

The sound of heels on the hardwood let me know Priscilla was headed down the hallway, right toward us. A jolt of adrenaline shot through me. Time seemed to slow as suspense hung heavy in the air, the imminent confrontation causing my whole body to tense with anticipation.

"What do we do?" I whispered.

Before Miss May had a chance to respond, Priscilla stepped into the room. Her eyes widened as she saw me. "Chelsea? What are you..." Her gaze landed on Mike and she rushed over to him. "Oh my God, Mike!"

Priscilla's gaze darted around the room, taking in the broken window, and the general chaotic scene. Her expression turned grim as she looked over to me. "You did this."

6

PRETTY AND PANICKED

I've been accused of murder more times than I'd like to admit.

Prior to that night at Mike's, the accusations had barely bothered me. But as I looked into Priscilla's eyes, I could tell she thought I'd committed the crime, and that scornful look attacked my insides with a sharp, painful burn.

Part of me felt defensive and angry. Priscilla didn't know me well, sure, but I'd established a reputation as someone with a deep devotion to justice. How could she think one of Pine Grove's acclaimed local sleuths could have killed Mike in cold blood? I think part of me also felt some version of pity. Poor Priscilla was doing her best to process the death of her fiancé. I felt bad that she had to deal with that.

Perhaps more than anything, I felt scared. Everyone in town knew Mike had broken my heart. Now he was dead, feet away from a note that implicated me, and I was in the room with the body.

Will this one send me to jail for life? I thought. *Or will we be able to catch the killer and establish my good name once and for all?*

"Priscilla." Miss May stepped toward the shaking woman like she was approaching a trapped cat. "We're just as shocked as you are."

"That's what you *would* say. You're the aunt of the killer." Priscilla's eyes cut back over to Mike. Her bottom lip quivered, and her nostrils flared. "Mike!"

She fell to her knees beside the body, sobbing. I winced as she placed a palm down in the blood pooled beside the body, but refrained from pointing it out. This was the first investigation where we'd born witness to a loved one discovering the corpse. My heart swelled with compassion as Priscilla cycled through futile attempts at processing Mike's murder.

She said his name over and over. Checked for a pulse in his neck and both wrists. Lowered her ear to his chest to listen for a heartbeat. Rinse, repeat, repeat, repeat.

Priscilla was about to cycle through the whole routine for the fourth time when Miss May cleared her throat. "Priscilla."

Priscilla looked right at me, revealing eyes that had reddened ten shades in the intervening moments since I'd seen them last. "You were jealous, weren't you? You heard we announced our date and you couldn't take it. I'm younger than you. And more beautiful. And Mike didn't leave me like he left you!"

Technically they'd never made it to the altar, so no one would ever know if Mike was planning on leaving Priscilla like he'd left me. But I kept that observation to myself, doing my best to remain tactful and restrained.

"I'm so sorry this happened," I said. "But I didn't do it."

Without thinking, I glanced over at the letter that the killer had left behind to frame me. Priscilla tracked my eyes, clawed her way to her feet, and grabbed the letter off the end table. She read it aloud to herself, mumbling through fast-falling tears.

"I told him moving here was a bad idea," she said, under her breath. "I told him you'd be too jealous. How could you not be?"

For Priscilla, it seemed insulting me was an essential part of the grieving process.

"You were stalking me all day," she continued. "First, you just so happen to be the one to help us at the farm. Then you just so happen to be at *Grandma's* when we're there. You waited for me to go to kickboxing. Once you knew Mike was alone... You attacked."

"That is..." *Don't say insane, Chelsea. Don't say insane.*

"It's insane," said Miss May. "You were at our farm. And everyone knows we're always at *Grandma's*."

I expected Priscilla to respond, but she was shaking her head and muttering to herself, like she hadn't heard a word Miss May had said. "I told him I didn't want to move here. But—but he insisted. 'Pine Grove is majestic.' 'Small towns are so much more relaxing than the city.' 'We need the slow pace of life now more than ever.' 'We need this chance to unplug.' Blah blah blah!" She charged across the room and loomed over Mike's body. "Look at you now, Mike! You made us come back, and your stupid ex murdered you."

"I did not murder Michael Gherkin," I said. "Think about it. If I were going to murder him, don't you think I would have done it when he left me at the altar?"

"You were a mental weakling then," said Priscilla. "Solving murders has given you the strength to commit one."

"You know what, Priscilla, you're upset, and I completely understand," said Miss May. "I think we're all upset right now. But instead of going down these rabbit holes about who killed Mike and why, how about –"

Priscilla didn't look away from Mike's lifeless body. "Chelsea did it!"

"I really didn't," I said.

"Then why were you here?" Priscilla covered her mouth with both hands, as if realizing something for the first time. "You were having an affair with him!"

"Why would I bring my aunt to my affair?" I said.

"Then why were you here?" she insisted.

I told Priscilla about how I'd found Mike's wallet at *Grandma's* and come over to drop it off. Her look of disbelief expanded with every word I uttered, then she let out a big, mocking laugh.

"You think the fact that you have Mike's wallet is proof that you didn't kill him? You probably took it as a trophy or something. I bet you steal the wallets of all your victims. I bet if I go to your house and look under your bed, there's a shoebox filled with dead people's wallets. Yup! That's what you do. You're sick, Chelsea Thomas. You're sick and you're going away for a very, very long time."

Miss May and I exchanged dumbfounded looks. We both choked out a few syllables, but neither of us could find any words to express how Priscilla's outlandish tale had made us feel. A car drove by outside, casting long shadows across Priscilla's face, so half of her was in the dark and the other half was in the light.

She pulled out her phone and made a call. "Hello, Pine Grove Police Department. I'd like to report a murder."

7

FLOUNDERING FLANAGAN

*P*riscilla stepped out into the hallway to continue the call. The second she exited, Miss May turned to me with her eyes bugging out.

"Priscilla thinks you did it!"

"I know that," I said. "It kind of makes sense, I guess. But why would I have brought you?"

"You don't think I'd be a good accomplice?" Miss May asked. "I'm smart. My attention to detail is unparalleled. And I've learned a lot over the course of solving all these mysteries."

I ran my tongue over my teeth. "That's a good point. We've both seen so many murders, ranging from carefully planned, to poorly-executed. Why would we have done such a crummy job at this one?"

"Crime of passion," said Miss May. "You got over-whelmed by emotion, so you showed up unannounced and bonked him on the head."

"So you're suggesting this was an impulsive crime of passion that I invited my aunt along for? There's no way that theory is going to hold up." I peered out into the hallway, where Priscilla was pacing on the phone. "Do you think we can maybe go home now? I need a shower."

Miss May groaned, moving her head from side to side as though she were considering the option. "I think we need to stay, Chels."

"Because if we leave it will look suspicious?"

"Very."

"Fine. I doubt we'll be here long anyway. Once Wayne shows up—"

"You think your twerpy little boyfriend is going to come and save you?" said Priscilla. "Yeah, right. Nothing will get between you and your rotting guilt!"

"Wow, OK," I said. "Wayne has been called many things, but never a 'twerp.'"

I expected a retort from Priscilla, but her gaze had once again fallen on Mike's dead body. Tears filled her eyes. She turned away, bringing her fingers to her temples.

A floorboard creaked as I stepped toward her. "You know I never would have done this, right?"

"I don't know anything," she said. "He—he made me move here. You know that? Now he's gone and I don't have anyone. Almost no family, and my friends are all in the city."

I recognized a former version of myself in Priscilla. Mike could be so hard-headed. There had been many times where I'd accused him of 'making' me do one thing or another. Over the years I'd learned to take a bit more personal responsibility, though that moment was not the right time to deliver that message to Priscilla. Instead, I stood a few feet away, doing my best to take deep, measured breaths, hoping that my presence could somehow help calm her.

"I think it might be wise for the three of us to re-locate to another room in the house," said Miss May. There was a gentle lilt in her voice. I wondered if that lilt could be traced back to our Irish ancestors. What would they think if they could see us now?

Priscilla gathered herself, sniffling and then clearing her throat. Her heels clacked as she exited the den and headed down the long corridor. The hallway was lined with professional photos of Mike and Priscilla, hanging in black frames that reminded me of skeleton bones. In one photo, Priscilla draped herself over Mike's shoulders and looked into the camera with a charismatic smile. In another, the two stood facing the sunset over the Hudson River. My favorite photo showed Mike and Priscilla wearing elegant attire, standing arm and arm with one another in a field of flowers. I recognized a genuine smile on Mike's face in that photo. It was the smile I'd fallen in love with. The smile I would never see again.

We settled into a formal living room on the opposite side of the house. Maybe it's crazy, but I couldn't help but critique the décor choices as I sat there. Two floral couches faced one another in the center of the room. A cheap cuckoo clock collected dust in a far corner. The rug was from Target, I knew that for a fact, and it clashed with literally every other piece Mike and Priscilla had selected.

"This is a lovely room," said Miss May.

Priscilla, who had been looking out the front window toward the road, said nothing. I cut my eyes over to Miss May. She looked over at me, and gave a little shrug.

"You said you talked to Chief Flanagan down at the station?" said Miss May, angling her body toward Priscilla.

Priscilla gave a small nod.

"Odd that she's not here yet. We're less than a mile from the department. They usually show up much more quickly than this."

"You mean when you claim your other victims?" said Priscilla.

"Why would we wait around for the cops after killing *anyone*?" said Miss May.

"That's how you project innocence," said Priscilla. "You... You kill people. Then you 'solve' their murders. And you never get caught for anything."

Miss May sighed. Not even Priscilla seemed to believe what Priscilla was saying. I tried to empathize. She came home and found her fiancé dead. Wasn't it only natural for her to look for someone to blame?

"She's here! Good!" Priscilla hurried toward the front door as Chief Flanagan parked outside and headed up the front steps. Miss May and I followed a few steps behind. I flicked on the hallway light, trying to make the house a little less creepy. It didn't help much.

Priscilla opened the door with a dramatic flourish. "Finally, you're here!"

Chief Flanagan, typically ready with a barb and an accusation, had her nose buried in her phone. "Um... Yes." She slowly peeled her gaze from the phone and slid it into her pocket. "Miss Rios. Hi."

I leaned forward to get a better look at the Chief. Her eyes were not bright and alert as they usually were. Her long, red hair was tussled and looked unwashed. And her uniform — form-fitting and crisply ironed on any other day — looked loose and rumpled.

Had Chief Flanagan lost weight? And were those dark circles under her eyes? Listen, I loved to hate the woman (and she'd made it easy over the years), but concern welled up in the pit of my stomach.

What was going on with our Chief of Police? And could it have had anything to do with Mike's murder?

8

DARK AND WAYNEY

*W*e arrived back at the farm late that night, tires crunching over our gravel drive and sending up a plume of dust behind us. Christmas lights twinkled on the front porch like beacons from Christmas seasons long gone. I thought of my parents. They'd greeted me with smiles every Christmas morning, laughing as I ran from one present to the next in excitement. Life was simple then. Innocence was something I couldn't have recognized, and I'd had no idea how to appreciate.

Our metal trash can had blown over. My whole body tensed as I approached to pick it up, anticipating the cold of the metal on my bare skin. Stopping a few feet short of the can, I looked around at the orchard. Moonlight penetrated a dense field of apple trees, casting eerie shadows on the frosted ground. Branches broke the silence with creaking moans, their arthritic fingers reaching out in desperation. A sense of foreboding flooded my mind.

Was someone watching me from the shadows? Or was I just being paranoid?

"Chelsea."

I stumbled back with such surprise that I tripped over my feet and landed with a thud on the ground. Wayne approached, laughing.

"Whoa! Didn't mean to scare you."

I took his hand and pulled myself back to my feet, mumbling about my clumsiness.

"It's been a night, Wayne." Miss May plodded up the porch steps. "How'd you get here? Didn't see your car."

"Parked it out by the barn." Wayne looked down and kicked at the dirt. "I drove straight to See- Saw for a private session."

Miss May and I both laughed. Our tiny horse, See-Saw, was quickly becoming the most popular therapist in Pine Grove.

"I didn't know she took your insurance," I said, smiling.

"I paid cash," said Wayne.

"You coming in?" Miss May held the door open and gestured inside with her head.

Wayne looked over at me. I shrugged. "Hang out for a bit, but I'm getting ready for bed."

Wayne sat at my desk chair, slurping loudly from a cup of coffee, as I got changed in my closet. I was desperate to find out what had driven him to have a late-night chat with See-Saw. But Wayne wasn't always the most emotionally available guy. I knew I'd have to be gentle if I was going to get to the truth, so I came at the issue sideways.

"I don't know how you can drink coffee this late," I said, digging through my dirty clothes, looking for something presentable.

"Doesn't affect me." Sluuuuurp.

Just ignore the slurp, Chelsea. He's never gonna open up if you tell him he drinks like a disgusting animal.

"Uh-huh," I said. "You say that now, and tomorrow

you're going to complain that you woke up at three in the morning feeling wide awake."

Sluuuuurrrp.

"Was See-Saw doing OK tonight?" I said, attempting to inch closer to the truth.

"She was doing great." His voice was monotonous and dry.

Sluuuuuurp. My patience thinned.

"Wayne."

"What?"

I stuck my head out of the closet, clutching my chosen pajamas (a matching flannel set, if you must know) to my chest. "Anything you can say to my tiny horse, you can say to me. You know that, right?"

"Yeah, sure."

"Are you feeling weird because of Mike? I mean... it's totally crazy."

"What do you mean? What happened with Mike?" He sat up straight. "Did he do something to you?"

"What? No. How do you... You haven't talked to Flanagan? She was like a space cadet at the scene, but I thought she'd at least have a report filed by now."

"She sent me home early, didn't tell me why. That's how I ended up talking to See-Saw."

"If you weren't talking about Mike, what were you talking about?"

"The wedding," said Wayne.

My heart skipped a beat. Our wedding was just days away. I could not deal with a cold-footed fiancé. Wayne must have read the terror on my face because he immediately put that fear to rest. "I'm not worried about marrying you," said Wayne. "That's the best choice I've ever made."

My shoulders relaxed. I hadn't even realized I'd tensed them. "Then what's the problem?"

"There's no problem, Chelsea. Cute pajamas, by the way."

"Wayne."

"I want it all to go perfect, OK? There are so many moving parts. The church. Bussing the guests to the farm. The party favors. The music. What if—What if—You don't deserve another botched wedding."

"As long as I'm marrying you, none of that other stuff matters." I emerged from the closet and gave him a warm smile. "Now I need to tell you what happened with Mike."

Wayne listened carefully as I reported on the details of the Case of the Murdered Mike. I started with Mike's deplorable behavior up by the Christmas trees, then I hit the strange game of keep-away at the restaurant, and for the grand finale I described his dead body and the scene of the crime (probably in too much detail, which I'll avoid here).

There was a long pause after I finished describing Mike's murder. Wayne's forehead wrinkled as he sat there, thinking. I almost interjected to comment on how handsome he looked, then thought better of it (*time and a place, Chelsea*). Finally, Wayne looked up with clear eyes.

"Tell me what happened after Flanagan got there."

"Like I said before, she was a space cadet. When she showed up, she was scrolling on her phone, looking at something. She barely followed along as Priscilla lobbed accusation after accusation at me and Miss May."

"Flanagan didn't latch on to that stuff? She's usually the first to accuse you."

"Not this time. She just looked...lost. Like she barely knew where she was."

"That's been happening more and more lately," said

Wayne. "Whatever's going on with her is a mystery in its own right. None of the guys down at the station can figure it out."

"Pine Grove cops aren't really known for solving mysteries," I said.

Wayne rolled his eyes like, *very funny*. "Tell me what happened next."

"Nothing really," I said. "Flanagan took notes on everything Priscilla said. But when she was interviewing me and Miss May, she kept having us repeat ourselves. It was all so unlike her."

"And how are you feeling?" said Wayne. "I mean, Mike was a jerk, and he left you at the altar. But you almost married the guy."

"I want to find him justice." I narrowed my eyes and looked over at Wayne. "It's just so weird that Flanagan didn't debrief the department on Mike's murder."

"I turned off my phone when I was talking to the horse. I probably have a message from her." said Wayne.

"Turn it on."

Wayne did as he was told. He got hit with a notification bell as soon as the phone powered on. Then another, and another, and another. He swallowed hard.

"I better return these calls."

9

SCENT OF A MYSTERY

*T*he scent was rich and buttery, like a combination of scrambled eggs, cinnamon, and fresh-baked bread. It filled the entire house, and it dragged me out of bed by the nose like I was a marionette. Seconds later, I found myself floating toward the kitchen on my tippy toes, eyes half-closed in gentle anticipation.

As I got closer, I caught a hint of caramel mixed in with the swirling smells. Then came the warming smell of a fresh-brewed pot of dark roast coffee. Though I'm not proud of it, I'll admit to you that I moaned not once, not twice, but three times in a row.

Anyone would have.

Then, as I finally entered the kitchen, a smile crossed my face that otherwise only visited me on the massage table. Pure relaxation and anticipation, like I would fall asleep at any moment if not kept awake by the promise of what's to come.

On the center of the kitchen table sat a tower of French toast unlike any I'd seen in adulthood. Every slice was at least two inches thick. Gooey caramel dripped down the sides of the tower. Steam drifted off the top like snakes being awoken by a charmer.

"Oh, my goodness," I said, my voice sultry and low.

"She's smiling in ecstasy at the sight of me," said Teeny. "Not the first person who's done it, and doubtful she'll be the last."

My eyes drifted over to the stove, where Teeny stood with Miss May, grinning.

"I don't mean this as an insult in any way," I said. "But I literally had no idea anyone was in this room other than me and that pile of French toast. Caramel?"

"Let's call it a Caramel Crème Brûlée French Toast," said Miss May.

Teeny scoffed. "You are such a snob!"

"You're just jealous 'cuz you didn't come up with it," said Miss May.

"Of course, I'm jealous," said Teeny, suddenly getting very serious. "You'll tell me the recipe, right?"

"Honestly, it was so easy." Miss May poured a few mugs of hot coffee and added cream and sugar as she spoke. "You start soaking the bread the night before – not too much though! - then pop them in the oven in the morning and you've got one of the most decadent treats ever, without doing much work at all."

"Soak it in what?" Teeny emphasized 'what' like she was furious Miss May hadn't provided more detail.

I hurried over to the leaning tower of toast and yoinked off the top slice with my thumb and pointer. "Can I guess?"

Miss May gestured, like, *go right ahead.*

I took a bite. Oh. My. Smoking. Blazing. Trumpeting. Chaotic. Goodness. There was an incredible brown sugar crust on top that crunched in my mouth. Then it all melted together into a decadent, gooey treat that was moist, chewy and oh-so-rich. "Whoa."

"Is that all you got?" said Teeny.

"Don't judge me. It was the only word I could muster in the midst of a life-changing experience."

Miss May laughed. "What do you taste."

I took another bite. Oh. My. Smoking. Blazing... *OK. You get the idea*. "Eggs. Milk. Cream.Vanilla. And salt! Can't forget the salt."

"Missing one ingredient," said Miss May, grinning.

"Rum!" I turned to see that Teeny had chewed through most of an entire slice in the preceding moment. "There's rum in here!"

"Ding, ding, ding!" said Miss May.

"If my ex-boyfriend gets murdered will you make *me* something special like this the morning after?" said Teeny.

"If I say 'yes' does that mean you're going to kill one of your exes?" said Miss May.

"Absolutely." Teeny took another huge bite of French Toast. "It'd probably be one of the Rons."

A few moments later, the three of us were settled at the table, enjoying Miss May's creation. That's right. We'd managed to sit down and eat at the same time. Please. Hold the applause. We spent the first portion of the meal gushing over the French Toast, then Miss May got down to business.

"We need to figure out how to start this investigation," she said. "And I think I have an idea."

"Go on..." I said, swallowing a big bite.

"Priscilla showed up before we got to do a complete sweep of the scene of the crime," said Miss May.

Teeny leaned forward. "Me and your aunt think we need to get back in there and see what we can find. But there's a problem."

She looked over at Miss May, who continued, "I drove by early this morning. Flanagan has Hercules stationed at the house along with some other deputy. I don't think we're going to be able to sneak past them."

"What do we do then?" I said.

Miss May gave me a tight little smile. "We're thinking you can call Wayne. Maybe he can tell us when they're having a changing of the guard over there and we can slip inside between shifts."

"Wayne didn't even know Mike had been murdered 'til I told him last night," I said.

"So what?" said Miss May.

I sighed. Those two little words were all Miss May needed to dismantle my weak argument. "Fine. I'll call him after my next slice."

Miss May slid the house phone toward me. "How about you call him now?"

Stepping out onto the porch, I zipped up my coat and dialed Wayne's number. Riiiiing. Riiiiiiiing.

"You're up early."

I smiled. "Caramel Crème Brûlée French Toast."

"Say no more. Hey, we're meeting with the florist later, right?"

I widened my eyes. Wayne and I had an appointment with our wedding florist for later that morning. If he hadn't reminded me, I never would have been there. "Wouldn't miss it for all the pie in the universe," I said.

"You forgot about it 'til I just brought it up?"

"Yup."

"C'mon, Chels. This is important. Honestly, I'm kind of worried about it. Mrs. Geyer hasn't replied to any of my messages. And if she doesn't do the arrangements right, it's not going to be perfect, and you deserve a perfect –"

"Wayne. We talked about this last night. Nothing needs to be 'perfect'. It's a big event. One or two things might go wrong. But you and I are getting married! There's nothing to worry about."

"OK. Fine. Thanks."

"Anything for you, Detective," I said. "You big, beautiful, handsome, kind, helpful, generous, *helpful* man."

"Uh-oh," said Wayne. "You need something from me. What is it?"

I winced. Wayne hadn't solved a single murder in Pine Grove, but he'd been oddly perceptive of late. He remained quiet as I asked him to sneak us back into Mike's house. Once I'd gotten the request out, he met it with a long, deep sigh.

"I know it's not going to be easy," I said. "But we need your help here."

"I would help you if I could," said Wayne. "But I can't."

"What do you mean?"

"Flanagan barred me from working on the case."

10

FLOWERING DRAMA

I met Wayne outside Geyer's Flowers later that day. The flower shop was small-town cute, with beautiful bouquets in the windows and a hand-painted sign hung above the door. The only element of the tableau that wouldn't have fit in a Norman Rockwell painting was Wayne himself.

My guy was pacing back and forth in front of the shop like a caged beast, muttering to himself, shaking his head every few seconds. He didn't even notice when I pulled up in my hot, hot muscle car. Nor did he notice when I got out, stared at him, took a video, and texted the video to him.

Leaning forward, I tried to catch a word or two of his utterances. Couldn't grab much other than the occasional 'unbelievable' or 'what the...' Finally, I climbed on a nearby bench, cupped my hands around my mouth and bellowed: "Detective Wayne Hudson, you're under arrest!"

Was it foreshadowing? Dramatic irony? Let's hope not...

Wayne looked up at me with a start. "Holy Chelsea!"

"Oh, have I been sainted now?" I held out my hand and he helped me down from the bench. We hugged. I felt his big heart beating through his big chest. "What's going on with you? I've been watching you freak out for like, five minutes. Now it feels like you're going to have a heart attack."

"What do you mean you've been 'watching' me?" said Wayne. "It didn't occur to you that I might need help? Maybe talking to a little horse is all *you* need, but sometimes human interactions can be beneficial, too."

"Please don't besmirch the name of my tiny therapist," I said. "And I'm sorry. I didn't think you were, like, in a crisis."

Wayne sighed and looked away. "I'm not. It's just... I've never been taken off a case like this before."

"Flanagan has it out for you."

"This is coming down from the 'regional commissioner,' whatever that is. She says she wishes she could help but it's out of her hands. I didn't even know we had a regional commissioner."

"Me neither. Does this person actually exist or is it possible she's messing with you?"

"Oh, he exists," said Wayne. "And so does his big, stupid, salt n' pepper mustache. This guy is ridiculous, Chelsea. He's all short and squat and he's got one of those complexes. Nepalese Complex."

"It's called a Napoleon Complex," I said, hoping Wayne wouldn't mind my correction compulsion.

He pointed right at me. "That! Exactly. This little guy makes up for his tininess by growing a huge mustache and throwing his weight around. Says I have a conflict of interest so I can't look into Mike's death."

I moved my head from side to side. *Now is not the time to side with Napoleon, Chelsea... But... But... But...* "I mean, he's not totally wrong."

"What!? Chelsea. The only reason I should be taken off

this case is if I am not capable of looking at the crime objectively. Yeah, my future wife had a bad history with the guy. But I'm a professional. I can look past that in order to do my job right."

"I know—"

"But you agreed with Napoleon! You're a Napoleon sympathizer."

Wayne threw up his hands and snorted air out his nose in such a comical way I couldn't help but laugh. My laugh softened him, and he laughed too. "Quit it."

"I'm sorry. You're cute when you're enraged. I know you can do your job no matter what, but I can see the guy's logic, that's all."

Wayne kicked some loose gravel off the sidewalk, kept shaking his head in what appeared to be dismay. "Apparently, he's been making Flanagan's job impossible ever since she got here."

"Seriously?" I said. "This guy has been around *that* long? How have you not met him before?"

"She says she was trying to keep the rest of us from having to deal with his nonsense, and he was too lazy to come into the precinct. Well, he's not lazy anymore. And his dumb cheddar cheese sandwich has been on my desk all day."

I laughed. "Alright. I'm sorry you're going through all this with Commissioner..."

"Tate. Commissioner Edward Tate. What kind of guy is named Edward and doesn't go by Ed? How was this guy ever a beat cop? I don't get it."

"I know. But the way I see it, this means you're freed up to help on my investigation, as long as you keep it on the down low. And we're here to do a fun wedding thing. Do you think you can drop the Tate hate so we can finalize the flowers for our wedding this weekend? We're getting married very soon, Detective Beeferson."

"That's not my name," Wayne took my hand in his, "and I can never drop the Tate Hate. But I can keep it to myself for now."

"Perfect."

I gave him a quick kiss on the cheek and spun on my heels, entering the flower shop with a bubbly smile. The smile faded once I was a few feet into the shop. I'd expected to see ol' Mrs. Geyer trimming flowers, humming to herself in a wonderland of greens, pinks, purples and blues. What I saw instead was ol' Mrs. Geyer surrounded by moving boxes, with nary a flower in sight.

"Hi, Chelsea," she said, taping up one of the moving boxes. She sounded glum, and her green eyes were blood-shot and framed by dark circles.

"What's going on in here?" I said. "Is everything OK?"

"You didn't get my voicemail?"

I stammered. "I saw you called, but I didn't listen to the voicemail. Figured you were just confirming our appointment for today."

She sighed. "Why don't you young folks listen to your voicemails?"

"If it's important, most people follow up with a text." My heart caught in my throat as my thoughts sprang out ahead of me like bucking broncos. *Had Mrs. Geyer been crying? Had there been another murder in town? Were her family members OK?*

I know. It's not healthy to jump to tragic conclusions just because your florist seems dismayed. But after years of solving murders, it was hard to keep myself from going to the cobwebbed corners of my mind.

"My fingers are too big for texting." Mrs. Geyer held out her normal-sized hands. I had no retort.

"What's going on, Mrs. G?" said Wayne.

"What does it look like?" Mrs. G gestured around the flower shop. "I'm closing up shop."

"Wait. What?" I blinked a few times. "What do you mean?"

"My sister bought a place in Florida and said I can live with her for free. I'm gonna miss this place," she sniffled, "but it's time."

"Okay..." I dragged out the word, demonstrating confusion and a touch of annoyance. "What does that mean for our wedding flowers?"

Mrs. Geyer hung her head and rubbed her eyes. A tear slid down her cheek, falling to the gray carpet like a tiny little meteor, crash landing on my hopes and dreams.

"I'm sorry. I can no longer help with that."

"This is so insane," I said, stepping outside with Wayne.

"It's ridiculous. And it's exactly what I was afraid of," said Wayne.

"What are we going to do?" I said.

"I'll fix it. But first... There's something else I've got to do."

"What?"

Wayne turned to me with a sharp look of determination. "You still need help sneaking into Mike's place?"

"How did what happened in there lead you to want to help me with the case?"

"I'm tired of being jerked around, and I want to do something useful," said Wayne. "You want to get into that house or not?"

11

OPEN MIKE

I stopped the T-bird a few houses down from Mike's and I killed the lights. Craning my neck, I saw that a cop was still stationed out front of the big, brick home. Teeny stuck her head into the front seat, wedging it between me and Miss May.

"What's that guy doing there? I thought this was our moment!"

"Our moment isn't for another few moments." Miss May turned to me. "Wayne says this guy will slink off early to get to *D'Avola's* before they close for the night, right?"

"Yup," I said, "and this is our only chance, because Hercules comes next and he takes his sentry position very, very seriously. Wayne says he's actually been making the other cops refer to him as a sentry or sentinel all day."

"Small towns attract the strangest police officers," said Miss May. "No offense, Chelsea."

Teeny flopped back in her seat and did her little Teeny golf claps, tittering with excitement. "Oh, I love a good stake out! What if we pass the time by rolling our own cigars, and then we each take a puff, and it turns out we hate them so we throw them out the window? I bet the experience will bond us, despite how unpleasant the cigars will be."

"*North Port Diaries*, *Blood and Bones*, or *Jenna and Mr. Flowers*?" I said.

"You got me," said Teeny, laughing. "That was a scene in an early episode of *Jenna and Mr. Flowers*. Mr. Flowers, you know, he's so particular. Well, he pretended he smoked cigars just to seem tough in front of Jenna. She went out and got the cigar guts or whatever, the stuff you need to roll your own. Then they were on a stakeout and—"

"Shh!" I leaned forward, squinting, as someone pulled up to Mike's place. "Oh no! That's the delivery car from *D'Avola's*. If this cop gets his pizza delivered, there's no chance he's leaving early."

Without thinking, I started the T-bird and drove up to the delivery car, boxing the driver in by pulling up real close to his door. Seconds later, Jerry D'Avola, the teenage son of Pine Grove's first family of pizza, rolled down his window. He had slicked back hair and was wearing a crisp polo shirt emblazoned with the shop's logo.

"Hey! You're boxing me in. I gotta make a delivery."

I leaned across Miss May. "Jerry, it's Chelsea, Teeny, and Miss May."

"Unless there's another dead body in that house, you need to let me through."

"We can't let you deliver pizza to that cop," I said. "Drive away, then call him in a few minutes and tell him you got a flat."

"Dad's gonna kill me if I get a flat," the kid said.

"Don't actually get a flat, just tell the cop you got one. Tell him you can't do any deliveries tonight, so he's got to come into the shop to pick up his pizza like he usually does."

"Ohhhh," Jerry said. "I get it. You want to pull him off of this house so you can go inside and do your dirty work."

"We don't do 'dirty' work," I said. "But yeah. We need to poke around the scene of the crime, and that's only going to happen if you get a flat tire."

"But these tires are new!"

"Jerry. Don't get a real flat. Come on, stay with me here."

It took a few more minutes of conversation (plus a $50 bribe), but Jerry D'Avola finally agreed to our plan. Once he was gone, we resumed our stakeout. I broke into a huge smile as the cop hurried out of the house and into his squad car. And we slipped inside through the back, just as we had before.

Miss May led the way to the den as I did my best to avoid looking at Mike's gross, nasty, no-good furniture.

"How long do we have in there before Hercules shows up?" she asked.

"Ten minutes, tops," I said.

"Alright. We all need to work efficiently. Search every inch of that room. But put everything back where you found it. No one can know we were in there."

Once inside the den, a golf club resting on the bookshelf caught my eye. There was a dark stain on the thick, metallic head of the club. My hands clammed up as I dropped to my knees to investigate further. I swallowed hard. Mike had always loved golfing. It would have been so tragic if he'd been killed by one of his trusty clubs. "Miss May? Is this blood?"

"Looked like mud to me," she said, without looking over from a credenza she'd been investigating. "See how there's a small clump of grass embedded into the stain? That wouldn't be there if you were looking at the murder weapon."

"You already clocked this club?" I said.

She nodded. "Spotted it on the way in. Keep searching. We don't have much time."

"This glass was broken from the inside," said Teeny, lingering near the broken window. There aren't any shards of glass in this room, but I can see a couple tiny pieces suspended in the bush outside."

"What do we think that means?" said Miss May.

"Signs of a struggle, for one thing," I said. "But also... It's a sign that Mike invited his killer inside the house. They didn't have to break the window to get in."

"We slipped in twice without having to break anything," said Miss May.

"That's because Mike had just unlocked the door for whoever did this to him," I said. "Trust me. The guy was paranoid about security. He never came in without locking the door behind him. He even had a safe he never gave me access to..."

I trailed off as a thought occurred to me.

"What?" said Teeny.

I crossed the room, where a print of an old *Goldfinger* poster hung framed on the wall. Mike had bought the poster at a Brooklyn flea market when the two of us were together. I'd always teased him because he'd never seen the movie. He'd insisted one could appreciate art without knowing the story behind it, and had displayed the poster prominently in his study.

Mike didn't tell me why he'd *really* bought the poster for months. Then one day, after we'd gotten engaged, he removed the poster from the wall with a grin. "James Bond is the only man fit to guard the king's most treasured valuables." I'd stepped forward to see that the poster had been hung in front of a huge wall safe that I'd had no idea existed.

I'd begged Mike to tell me what was in the safe, but he'd refused with a smug, satisfied grin.

"What did you realize?" said Teeny, snapping me back to the present moment.

"You'll see."

I gingerly grabbed the poster by either side of the frame. It lifted off the wall much more easily than I'd expected. Behind it was the same wall safe Mike had had installed in our New York apartment, with one notable difference. This time, the safe was wide open, and no one was there to stop me from finding out what was hidden inside.

12

SO MANY SUSPECTS

"Whoever killed him must have emptied that safe." I climbed out of the T-bird and headed toward the farmhouse.

"Or Mike had emptied the safe a while back and this is just a coincidence," said Miss May. "You sure you can't remember what he used to keep in there?"

"I can't remember something I never knew," I said. "Sometimes I thought he kept it empty, and only had it installed so he could feel important."

"If that's true, then the safe isn't related to this case at all," said Miss May. "But the empty safe and the dead body feel connected."

I climbed the back porch and entered the kitchen. Steve the dog jumped up on me as soon as I got inside. I stumbled back a couple steps, laughing. "Good to see you too, fine sir!"

His reaction? More jumping and licking. He calmed down a bit as I squatted down and petted him behind his ears. "Well, you feel so soft today. What's that about? Huh? Are you extra soft or am I crazy?"

A gruff male voice boomed from nearby. "I groomed him!"

Our farmhand, KP, emerged from the den. He was wearing sweatpants and a *Pine Grove High School* sweatshirt, drinking from a mug that was shaped like Santa's bearded face. It wasn't uncommon to find KP in the farmhouse at odd hours. He was a member of the family like that. But he'd never surprise-groomed Steve before.

"You must have gotten real lonely in that cabin over there if you popped by the farmhouse to groom Steve," said Miss May.

"Naw," said KP in his country drawl. "Just figured there's only room for one stinky old dog on this farm, and I didn't want to be the one to shower. How's that car holding up, Chels? Still better than the one I got you?"

I chuckled. KP had gifted me a beat up old pickup a while back, and it had served me well. The truck had broken down while he'd been away, and then the towns-people had gifted me the T-bird. KP's ego still hadn't recovered.

"Oh, so much better," I said, rolling my eyes. "Thank goodness that junky pickup finally bit the dust. I'd been dying to get rid of it forever."

"Alright, alright, enough jokin' around," said KP. "You big meanie. Hey, speaking of which, what's up with your dead evil ex?"

"KP. Don't be callous." Miss May looked over at me. I knew she was checking to make sure I was holding up OK. It's the same look she gave me after my parents died. The same look she gave me after I got left at the altar. *Hold up. Has my life been weirdly tragic?*

"It's fine," I said, turning on the coffee pot to make a few cups of decaf. "KP, we're just about to talk about the murder. You want to weigh in on the details?"

"Nope." KP scooped up Steve and headed out the door. "But I'm stealing your dog for my movie night!"

Miss May and I laughed as he breezed out, talking to Steve like they were a couple of good ol' boys from back at the factory. Once he'd cleared out, I turned to Miss May and my smile faded.

"Too bad all of life can't be big, silly men and their little silly dogs, huh?"

Her smile faded right along with mine. "I'm still thinking about that empty safe."

I nodded. "Me too. Decent chance the empty safe and the murder are connected."

"And there's a great chance that this criminal is someone both you and Mike knew," said Miss May.

"You mean 'cuz he got killed and I got framed?" I asked. "I guess I was thinking I got framed because it was the easy choice. I mean, everyone knows I had plenty of motive to want Mike dead. But now that you mention it..."

"Decent shot the killer wanted to take you down, too."

A shiver ran to the tips of my fingers. I shook my arms and blew out a big breath. "Well, that's not charming at all."

Miss May chuckled. "It's certainly not."

"It's possible they framed me out of convenience though, right? I mean, it's not like I've *definitely* got some enemy out there who is waiting with bated breath for me to go to jail... 'Cuz, I mean, if I don't get locked up for this and the killer wanted to hurt me..."

"They might try to kill you next," said Miss May. "I've been wrestling that thought all day."

"OK, then." I exhaled and waited a few seconds for my

nerves to calm. "Mike had plenty of enemies. Let's run through them."

"Family?"

"Wealthy, arrogant, and entitled. They despised him, they despised each other, they despised themselves."

"No obvious suspects there?"

"They're all pretty terrible but none ever struck me as murderous." The coffee finished brewing. I poured myself a cup then held the pot out to Miss May. "Decaf?"

"I'm OK." She sat at the kitchen table. "Could have been Priscilla, right?"

"I suppose. But if she killed Mike, why would she have come home with us still there?"

"Maybe she didn't know anyone was inside the house," said Miss May.

I shrugged. "I can't see any immediate reason she would have done it. Why now? They'd just announced their engagement, they'd just bought a great house..."

"Could have had something to do with their argument at the farm," said Miss May.

"No one murders their partner over a Christmas tree. And they had totally made up by the time they went out to dinner, remember?"

Miss May nodded. "You seemed like you were having an out-of-body experience during that little cute-couple explosion at the restaurant."

"I kind of was," I said. "But let me think about who else could have done this."

As I thought, I added a tablespoon of cream into my coffee. I wished for a moment I was brewing a truth serum instead of a cup of coffee. That would make every investigation so much easier. The cream dissolved slowly, and I thought back to all of Mike's friends and acquaintances I'd met over the years. "There was a guy named Frank that was pretty close with Mike. And he had a business partner named Steven, too. Mike and Steven were inseparable for a while there, then they kind of grew apart, I think."

"That could be something," said Miss May. "Any angry ex-girlfriends?"

"You mean other than me?"

"You make jokes like that you're going to end up in jail, Chels."

I held up my palms, acknowledging Miss May's point. "There was one girl, now that I think about it," I said. "Mike always called her 'Jealous Jenny.'"

"Good suspect?"

"Decent," I said. "But no matter who killed him, I can't make sense of the timing."

"I agree," said Miss May. "Who goes out murdering just a few days before Christmas? What do we do next?"

I dropped a sugar cube into my coffee with a satisfying plunk. "We watch me drink my coffee. And we think."

13

SEE-SAW THE TRUTH

*A*s I lay in bed that night, my mind wouldn't stop turning over the details of the case. Mike had stormed through life like a concert pianist playing Rachmaninoff's angriest piece. During our time together, I'd seen him make enemies of bus boys, doctors, friends, colleagues, associates and, well, me. But none of us in the big pool of "folks who hated Michael Gherkin" had killed him in the intervening years.

I reflected back on Mike's questionable ethics.

Every so often, he'd suggest we scam a client to increase the profit margins at our interior design business. Once he'd gone so far as to switch out a Persian rug with a "high quality replacement" so he could pocket the difference as extra profit for the company. I'd reacted with shock and horror, as one does when their boyfriend and business partner exposes the worst side of themselves. And I'd made things right with the client, tactfully, of course. But Mike had laughed it all off and pretended like he'd been joking around. I'd always wondered if he'd cheated any more of our clients without me knowing. And if he was willing to mess with our shared clients, who might he have swindled in his life before he met me, or in his private life?

You might be judging me right now. Perhaps you want to scream, "Chelsea! Why were you with this guy?" I was tempted to be just as critical of myself in the wake of Mike's death. But I'd done a lot of self-growth since moving to Pine Grove, and I knew better than to be hard on myself for who I was in the past. We all make mistakes in life. If we're lucky, we learn and grow from them. I was one of the lucky ones.

It was almost one in the morning when I finally sat up in bed, puffed out my cheeks and slumped my shoulders, giving up on the idea of falling asleep. Steve the dog groaned from his snuggly spot beside me. He seemed to be saying "Stop fussing already and just fall asleep!" But I was too worked up, and I knew there was only one solution.

There was a biting cold on the air that night, the kind that makes you think "It's not supposed to be this cold before Christmas!" so I walked double-fast toward the stables. Once I got in there, I flipped on the heat lamp, pulled a stool beneath the glowing coils, and greeted See-Saw.

She did not greet me back, per se. But she turned to face my direction, big brown eyes open and inviting, as they always were. When it comes to humans, I need a lot of prompting before I'll open up. But I don't need more than that one, permissive look before I spill my heart to See-Saw.

I started with my conflicted feelings about Mike. Tragic death of crummy ex. Haunted by memories of our messed up relationship. Blah, blah, blah. See-Saw barely responded to this stuff, but it helped me to vent it out to her.

When I turned the conversation to my wedding, which was just a few days away at that point, she smacked her lips in interest. I chuckled. "Oh, I get it, girl," I said. "You don't want me to think about the men of the past when I've got a perfectly good future waiting for me."

She smacked her lips again.

"You're right," I said. "I don't need to be caught up in the past or the future. The present moment has everything I need to be happy."

She stomped her feet. That's what she always did when I'd hit the nail on the horse's head. I reached out and pet her back, enjoying the feeling of her velvety softness on my fingers. See-Saw had an incredible amount of majesty for such a small creature, such grace and charm. With each stroke, a sense of tranquility washed over me, and I could feel time slow down in See-Saw's presence. She responded with gentle nuzzles and soft whinnies, reminding me of the magic that exists in all of us but can be especially strong in our furry friends.

"You two seem to be having a nice night." Wayne's voice was soft and friendly. I turned just as he stepped into the barn. "I was hoping I might find you here."

"You want couples counseling with the tiny horse?" I said.

He chuckled. "Thought you might be up, and I wanted to apologize for losing my cool lately. This commissioner, 'Edward,' is messing with me at work. And I'm totally preoccupied with the wedding. Feel like I haven't been there for you enough through this whole Mike thing. I mean... You were gonna marry the guy. You holding up OK?"

I took his hand. "I've processed my emotions with See-Saw. Thank you, though."

"You know you can talk to me too, right?" said Wayne. "I'm at least as emotionally available as that horse."

"But do you have access to the same sage wisdom?"

"Definitely not," said Wayne. "I take it back."

He walked over and pet See-Saw. She nuzzled against him just as she'd nuzzled against me, with a quiet calm that washed over the whole stable.

"You, Teeny, and Miss May are going to have to take the lead on this investigation, big time," said Wayne. "What with Flanagan checked out. And the commissioner pushing everybody around…"

"You want to help me figure out who we should question first?" I said. "Could use some professional insight."

Wayne looked over at me, rolling his eyes. "Let's not pretend I've caught any of the killers around here."

"I still value your opinion," I said.

Wayne nodded, still petting See-Saw. He turned to me. "What did you say Priscilla's alibi was?"

14

FIGHT FOR THE TRUTH

*B*y the time I woke up the next morning, the house was empty. Steve had already been fed. The coffee in the pot was colder than Lake George in January.

Steve trotted alongside me as I walked around the kitchen in a slow circle, feeling like Kevin McCallister from *Home Alone*. "What am I supposed to do now?" I said to Steve. "Set up a bunch of booby traps to make sure a cop with a golden tooth doesn't break in and steal all the fancy stuff in the house?"

Steve had not seen *Home Alone*. He did not appreciate the reference.

"We need to get you caught up on classic Christmas movies," I said, feeding him a nibble of kibble from my palm. "Although I don't know how many movies we'll be able to watch this year. Remind me again why I'm getting married Christmas day?"

He wagged his tail. I fed him more kibble. My eyes caught the time on the microwave clock and my jaw dropped open. It was almost eleven AM, and if I didn't hurry, I was going to miss breakfast at *Grandma's*.

When I got to the restaurant, there was a line of waiting customers streaming out the door. A crowd like that wasn't an uncommon sight around the holidays. Pine Grove attracted lots of NYC people who wanted a taste of small-town living around the holidays, and thanks to a few choice online write-ups, Teeny's restaurant was almost always their first stop.

How did I know they were city people? There were three childless couples with visible tattoos. Several additional couples pushed strollers. And every baby in every stroller was dressed like a rock star in ripped black jeans, black t-shirts, and trendy little booties.

Pine Grove babies don't dress like that. They dress like whatever is on sale at the big box stores. And most local parents drag 'em out of bed and bring 'em to *Grandma's* in footy pajamas, anyway.

I found my ladies hunkered down at our booth in the back of the restaurant. There was a huge plate of chocolate chip pancakes between them, and I arrived just as Teeny doused the pancakes in fresh maple syrup.

"We're eating extra late today because of you, sleepy-head," said Miss May, patting the seat beside her.

"Late night session with See-Saw and Wayne. Long story. But I think I know what we need."

"Butter?" Teeny flagged down my favorite waiter, Petey. "Can we get a metric ton of butter please, Pete?"

Petey's trademark smile faded into a deathly serious stare. "That's two thousand pounds of butter, boss. I don't think I can do that."

"Just bring a little dish of the good stuff," said Miss May. "Country style, whipped and creamy."

"Oh. Right." Petey blinked a few times, then stumbled off.

"Good kid, but sometimes he's denser than your terrible Christmas Fruit Cake," said Teeny, eyeing Miss May.

"You don't like any fruit cake," said Miss May. "People who like fruit cake love it how I make it."

"I wasn't talking about butter," I said, elbowing my way into the conversation. "I was talking about the m-u-r-d-e-r."

"You know the people who eat in my restaurant can spell, right?" said Teeny. "Word on the street, Humphrey won the Pine Grove Elementary spelling bee back in the 1830s."

I cast a quick look over at Humphrey, who was stationed at the booth beside us. He forked a bite of eggs then brought it to his mouth, carefully navigating around the newspaper he held in front of his face.

"I don't think he's that old," I said.

"He is too," said Teeny. "One time he showed me his birth certificate. It was written in stone!"

Miss May and I chuckled as Teeny tossed her head back in an uproar of laughter. "Oh. that was good! Was that good? Was that a top five joke of all time?"

"It was very funny," said Miss May, turning to me. "Chelsea. You were saying."

I leaned forward and spoke in a hushed whisper. The pile of pancakes looked up at me with puppy-dog eyes, but I resisted shoving my face in them and instead remained focused on the task at hand. "Priscilla said she was at kick boxing when Mike got murdered, remember?"

Miss May pointed right at me. "You're right!"

"I'm pretty sure there's only one kick boxing class offered in all of Pine Grove," I said, raising my eyebrows in self-satisfaction. "And I just so happen to have a great, lifelong relationship with the teacher."

"I have no idea who you're talking about," said Teeny. "But if I did, I bet I'd make another killer joke about it."

The smell of Master Skinner's dojo transported me back to my teenage years. Afternoons spent with my face pressed up against the blue mats, learning how to defend myself. Weekend mornings cleaning those same mats with fresh wash cloths, soap, and water. The comforting scent of well-worn karate uniforms, launderedcountless times yet still crisp and white. Years of training flashed before my eyes as we stood in the lobby, waiting for Master Skinner to emerge from his office, reminding me of endless kicks, punches, and the pursuit of personal growth.

"You sure Master Skinner does kick boxing in here now?" said Teeny, scrunching up her nose. "Place still looks like a dojo to me."

"Yup." I pointed at a stack of kick boxing bags across the room. "I know because he's tried to recruit me to the class a dozen times."

Master Skinner emerged from the back of the dojo with his hands on his hips. The guy hadn't aged a single day since he'd taught me decades prior. "Versatility is key, even for the most highly-trained black belts." He gave us a deep bow. "Welcome to my dojo. It has been far too long."

"We've been busy catching bad guys," said Teeny. "You know Chelsea uses your karate to take down killers all the time?"

"I've heard the rumors." He looked at me with his small brown eyes. "You make me proud, student."

I bowed my head to him. "Thank you for training me. But we're not here to talk about old times, tempting as that may be. We're here because we need you to help us on an investigation."

He narrowed his eyes. "Was the most recent victim killed with karate?"

"Not at all," said Miss May. "The killer used blunt force trauma. It was not martially artistic in the slightest."

"Then I am confused," said Master Skinner.

"One of our suspects claims that she was at a kick boxing class during the time of the murder," I said. "If we can place her here, we can check her off the list. But if we can't..."

"I see. You need me to betray the trust of one of my students..."

"Only because one of your students might be a killer," I said.

"Very well." He let out a long, slow breath. "Fight me. Win or lose, I'll give you the information you need."

My jaw dropped. "I..."

Master Skinner jumped into a fighting stance. I remembered the guy well enough to know I wouldn't be leaving without engaging him a bit. My legs trembled as I handed Miss May my purse and stepped onto the mat.

"I came out here to tell you that Chelsea just had a duel with her former master," said Teeny.

KP took off his winter hat and ran a hand through his thinning hair. "Well, I'll be. Did that little dojo dude up and kill somebody? Chelsea had to take him down?"

"He didn't kill anyone," said Teeny. "Insisted on a duel before he gave us the information we needed about a possible suspect."

"Mike's wife said she was at a kick boxing class at the dojo while Mike was getting killed," I explained.

"We thought we might catch her in a lie, but Skinner says she was there, kicking and boxing with the rest of the hotties," said Teeny. "Master Skinner says she's incredibly lithe."

"OK, he didn't say she was lithe," I said.

"Hold on now, ladies. I don't care about some lithe wife of a dead man. I care about what happened in the show-down. Student versus master. That's a classic karate movie trope. Did you teach him a thing or two now that you've used your skills against real killers?"

"He whooped her heinie from here to Baton Rouge," said Teeny. "It was close at first. Chelsea lunged into the fray with a righteous right hook. Hit the little guy square in the jaw. Then she slipped on her own flop sweat and it all went downhill from there."

"I didn't slip on my own flop sweat," I said.

"You kind of did." Miss May winced. "I saw the dollop cascade off your forehead, then I saw your foot hit it, then I saw you go spilling back."

"I don't sweat dollops!" I groaned. Yeah, I know. I used to complain about my excessive sweat all the time when I first got to Pine Grove. But I'd stopped obsessing over my sweat, and I didn't want to go back in time just to indulge my two elderly besties and their desire to have a laugh at my expense.

KP suddenly perked up and walked off toward the parking lot. "Gotta go!"

"Where are you going?" said Miss May.

"Someone just pulled up," he called back. "I'm gonna try and sell them two trees for the price of one."

"Nobody needs two Christmas trees," said Miss May.

"Not true," said KP. "Last year Martha Stewart had fifty-eight!"

Once KP had cleared out, the three of us were left alone, surrounded by Christmas trees. I spotted a tiny snowflake drifting between the trees and looked up with a smile.

"It's snowing," I said.

"That's convenient. Maybe you can use the snow to soothe your aching bones after getting your booty beat by the Skin-man." Teeny tossed her head back and laughed. Miss May rolled her eyes and trudged away. "Aw, you're no fun. Where are you going?" said Teeny.

"Hot cocoa," said Miss May, without looking back. "See ya!"

Teeny and I exchanged urgent glances – *we didn't want to miss out on hot cocoa* – and we hurried after Miss May at double speed.

Moments later, the three of us were gathered around a little table in the bake shop, sipping at the edges of our cocoa, waiting for our drinks to cool. On that afternoon, the bake shop was as charming as it had ever been. The smell of nutmeg and cinnamon drifted off a tray of oatmeal cookies Miss May had prepped that morning. Frost covered the windows, letting in just the right amount of afternoon sun. Hidden speakers piped in my favorite Christmas tunes, sung by Frank Sinatra and Dean Martin.

Miss May plucked a baby marshmallow out of her drink and tossed it in her mouth. "Still can't believe Priscilla spent all night at that kick boxing class," she said.

"I believe it," said Teeny. "You don't get a hot little kick boxing bod without doing the actual kick boxing."

"What do we do now?" I said, eager to avoid further discussion of Priscilla's hotness.

"Seems to me it would still help to have a chat with Priscilla," said Miss May. "Our conversation over Mike's dead body was not the most civil. I think if we can approach her with the right energy, she might be willing to help us track down the killer."

"Not a bad idea," I said. "I mean, I know who all of Mike's old enemies were. But the way he lived, he probably picked up a dozen fresh ones in the past year alone."

My phone buzzed with a text. I read it, tossed back my head and groaned.

"What's up?" said Miss May.

"Wayne just texted. He said he's contacted every florist in the county and none of them can do our wedding on such short notice."

Teeny shook her head and 'tsk'd.' "Can't believe Mrs. Geyer did you dirty like that. I'd expect more decorum from a flower lady."

"I agree," said Miss May. "Petunia might have been gruff, but she never would have left one of her customers with no flowers a few days before her wedding."

"Too bad she took off to SoCal to pet a bunch of dogs." Teeny sipped her cocoa. I could tell it was still too hot, but she took another big sip anyway. That's how she lived, and that's why I loved her.

"She didn't go there just to 'pet dogs.' She's grooming

dogs," said Miss May. "And she's solving murders, too. I know you remember that."

Teeny rolled her eyes and took another sip of her too-hot cocoa.

"Just wait for it to cool, Teeny," said Miss May. "Snack on the marshmallows while you wait."

"I don't want to wait!" Teeny took another giant sip. Her eyes bugged out and she stuck her tongue out. "Ow! Ouch! Darn!"

Miss May and I made amused eye contact as we enjoyed tiny sips from our drinks.

"Don't you look at each other like that," said Teeny. "I see you!"

"No one's looking at anyone like anything," said Miss May. "What's the deal with Priscilla?"

"I vote we talk to her at Mike's memorial service tomorrow. Maybe his old friend Steven will be there, too."

Miss May crinkled her forehead. "Steven?"

"I think I mentioned him before," I said. "Steven was one of Mike's best friends back in the day. They did everything together. They'd run a few businesses together. I think they went to college together, too. Something like that."

"You think this Steven guy might have insight into the case?" said Teeny.

I nodded, biting my bottom lip. "It's also possible we should add Steven to our list of suspects."

"You just said they were big boy besties!" said Teeny.

"Yeah..." I looked away as I recalled a bitter current that had run between the two men. "Just something to consider, that's all."

15

MORNING GLORY

*T*eeny darted up to KP out in the middle of the pines just to tell him about my fight. "KP! You gotta hear this!"

"I gotta sell Christmas trees, is what I gotta do." KP turned to Miss May. "Last year this time we'd sold seven more trees than we have this year."

"That's natural variance," said Miss May. "It's the end of the season. I think we're safe to enjoy the lead up to Christmas without worrying about seven trees."

"I don't wanna lose out to last year's trees." KP's face reddened. "I hate losing, and I hate losing to past versions of myself more than anything. Future me has to beat past me into the dirt, or right now me gets mad."

"You're confusing me, and I'm usually the confusing one," said Teeny. "Plus, wasn't every version of you a future you at some point?"

"And every future you will one day become a past you, too," I said with a grin.

"Why'd you come out here all excited? Just to boggle my mind with your philosophical quandaries?" said KP.

16

FACE-ING THE ENEMY

*M*ike grew up in the adjacent town of Blue Mountain, NY. The memorial was held at the funeral home there. Housed in an old colonial, painted white with black shingles, the place was tastefully decorated for the holidays with white icicle lights and the iron silhouettes of trumpeting angels staked into the yard.

It was so cold that morning that my wet hair had frozen on my walk from the house out to the car. Thankfully, my hair had dried by the time we made it to the funeral home, and the frozen parts had developed pretty waves.

Note to self: start a 'hair-freezing salon' to help women achieve the natural waves they've always wanted. Call it 'Ice and Easy.' Make millions.

Teeny hurried toward the funeral home with her hands buried in her pockets. After a few steps, she broke into a little trot.

"Why are you running?" said Miss May.

"Don't have enough meat on my bones to survive this cold too long!" Teeny called back.

I looked over at Miss May as I zipped my coat all the way up. "Did Teeny just accuse us of having meat on our bones?"

"Less of an accusation, more of an observation," said Miss May. "Before we go in there, I think I have a moral obligation to ask... Are you sure you want to do this? The last time you saw Mike's relatives gathered, wearing their nicest clothes—"

"Was my wedding, I know," I said. "The thought has occurred to me. But I'm done re-living the past. I'm all about being right here, right now. And I have nothing to be ashamed of. If anything, they should be ashamed of *him*!"

"They'll probably be too caught up grieving his tragic and senseless murder to be ashamed of him, but I get your point," said Miss May.

I stepped into the foyer of the funeral home, unzipping my coat. The place smelled of lilies. My heels clacked loudly against the wood floors. A huge photo of Mike watched me from its perch on an easel. In the photo, Mike was wearing business clothes, looking at the camera without smiling. The look in Mike's eyes was somehow both empty and angry, like he resented having his photo taken, and wanted nothing more than to reach out, smash the camera, and go along with his day.

"I want to say this is a bad picture of Mike," said Miss May, "But the photographer really managed to capture his essence."

"It's haunting me," I said, shivering. "That look in his eyes."

Teeny yanked at my sleeve. "Did you just say you're being haunted by this photo? That happened once on my paranormal mystery show. The poor woman was haunted at her husband's funeral *by* her husband. Can you believe that?"

"I didn't know you watched a paranormal mystery," said Miss May.

"Oh yeah. Sometimes I'm in the mood for *Other Worldly Whimsy*," said Teeny.

"What's the show called?" said Miss May.

"*Other Worldly Whimsy.* I just told you that."

Miss May lobbed back a gentle retort, and as the women bantered back and forth, I drifted into the adjoining viewing room. A casket rested at the front of the room. Closed. Covered in lilies. Several men and women were seated in chairs facing the casket. Though I hadn't planned on it, I approached the casket and kneeled.

Tears began a slow ascent from the pit of my stomach toward my eyes. I tried to halt them in my throat, but they continued upward until a few reached the shores of my eyelids. Though I blinked a few times, that did little to stop them. Before I knew it, I was quietly crying, hands clasped together in a praying posture, looking at the casket like it could somehow provide answers.

Only a few tears escaped before I regained composure. "Looks like you made me cry one last time, Mike." I spoke quietly, and with a lightness and love that surprised me. "I really wanted to marry you. You know that? We had our issues, sure. And maybe we weren't ready. Maybe you figured that out and that's why you never made it to the altar that day. But I wanted to meet you up there. I wanted to say, 'I do.' I wanted to kiss you in front of all the people we loved." My voice had begun to quaver. I took a deep breath then let it out. "What happened between us was for the best. I think we both grew after that disastrous attempt at a wedding. I know I did. And I could tell you had grown, too. That was clear, just from the few times I'd seen you around town. We'd both learned that responsibility can be a good thing, I think."

Suddenly I felt the presence of someone lurking a few feet away, awaiting their turn at the casket. As I released a second deep breath, I realized I felt a sense of relief. Perhaps I'd been waiting all those years to have some closure with Mike. Too bad the conversation hadn't happened until he'd died. But you can never control the uncertainty of life, so there's often no choice but to roll with the punches (or murders, as is so often the case in Pine Grove).

I stood and scanned the room, looking for a place to sit. Mike's parents were there, heads bowed, and shoulders slumped. Also present were a couple of aunts and uncles I recognized, along with a few cousins I'd gotten to know briefly before the botched wedding. Mike's old friend Frank was there. And so was a young woman I thought *might* have been his ex, 'Jealous Jenny.'

As my eyes darted across the dimly lit room, a chill crawled up my spine. Soft, yellow lights cast distorted shadows on the faces of the mourners, each one a potential suspect hiding behind an inscrutable mask of innocence. With each passing moment, the gravity of the situation weighed on me further. Anyone in that room could have killed the man we'd all gathered to mourn.

For reasons unknown to me at the time, Mike's best friend Steven was not in attendance. And neither was Priscilla Rios.

17

FRANKEN FACTS

*M*iss May leaned over to me as I grabbed the seat next to her. "Where's Priscilla?"

I shrugged. "Can't believe she's not here." A tense unease creaked in my stomach like an orchestra tuning before a big performance. "And she's not the only one who's missing. Mike's former business partner and best friend Steven isn't here either."

Miss May nodded toward the young blonde woman I'd spotted at the front of the room. "Is that Jealous Jenny?"

"I think so, but I can't be sure," I said. "Maybe—"

"Shh." Miss May pointed to the front of the room, where a priest was getting settled behind a small podium.

The priest eulogized Mike impersonally, referencing Mike's academic and work accomplishments, but not much else. Mike's mother, Veronica Gherkin, sobbed throughout the eulogy, only stopping to mutter "why?" or groan with indignant anger. I was careful not to stare, though several other mourners took no such care, gawking freely in her direction and dabbing their own tears with pocket squares and Kleenex.

The overall vibe of the crowd could be described as 'modern aristocrats.' Though Blue Mountain is a blue-collar town, the Gherkins were an exception to the demographic norms, one of few families who had a house up on the mountain overlooking the town and into the horizon for miles. Mike and I had connected over our neighboring small towns on our first date, and I'd often wondered why he hadn't chosen Blue Mountain when he and Priscilla had made their great migration away from New York City.

Anyway, back to the aristocratic mourners. Several older men were outfitted in bespoke suits. I imagined they were friends of Mike's father from the world of New York City finance. Each of these men came with wives much younger than them, soaked in diamonds, pearls, and a haughtiness uncommon in Blue Mountain. There were also a handful of younger men and women, also dressed in fine clothes. I recognized a few as Mike's friends from Yale. Another was Mike's former partner from his stint working in banking. Mike's friend, Frank, sat separate from the other Millennials in attendance, though he too was dressed like he was headed to a wedding that would be photographed for *People Magazine*.

I caught up to Frank in the parking lot after the service. Figured he might have information about Steven's conspicuous absence, and I wanted to pick his brain about Priscilla, too.

He was about to climb into a waiting town car but stopped when I called his name. As I got closer, I noticed deep, dark circles under Frank's eyes. He was also skinnier than he'd been the last time I'd seen him. He'd grown a patchy beard and blinked with a nervous twitch.

At first, we made small talk. Frank and I had been friends, through Mike, for years. Frank said he was glad to see me, and it seemed like he meant it. I responded in kind, paying him a compliment or two about his suit, asking about his family and what he'd been up to. Miss May and Teeny circled us, acting like they were chatting with one another, but they each glared at me like *get down to business, girl!*, so after a while I felt I had no choice but to bring up the investigation.

"Hey Frank, you know I'm a sleuth now, right?"

He nodded. "Sometimes articles about you come up on my Facebook. I know, I know. Facebook is for old people. But I'm getting old, and I accept it. Besides, how else was I supposed to find out what was up with you?"

"You could have asked Mike. Especially after he moved to my small town with his fiancée."

Frank chuckled. "For the record, I told him that was a bad idea. But he was like, 'Find me a better town within a decent drive to Manhattan and I'll live there.' I couldn't find anything, so he moved up. That simple. Was it weird for you?"

"The most I saw of him since he moved to town was when I discovered his dead body." I winced. "Sorry. That was insensitive."

"You gotta be able to make dark jokes like that in life," said Frank. "I try to find humor in everything. Otherwise, what's the point, you know?"

I nodded. "Can I ask you something?"

"You want to know why Jenny showed up to the memorial?"

"No, but—"

"The two of them reconnected in the past year or two. Patched things up. I guess Mike wanted to make nice with all his exes before he got hitched."

"He never reached out to me," I said.

Frank shrugged. "He moved to your tiny town and started making nice with all your neighbors."

"Hadn't thought of it like that," I said. "Why isn't Priscilla here today? Were you friends with her?"

"I didn't know her that well, but I heard some people talking about it. Sounds like she was too upset. Had to leave town for a bit, hit up a retreat upstate or something. Massage, cold plunge, hot tub, that kind of thing. You gotta do what you gotta do for your mental health, right?"

"Did Mike's family get along with her?"

"Oh, they loved her. It was a beautiful thing. Mike's mom and Priscilla had a private text thread. Priscilla golfed with Mike's dad. I'm telling you – it was special and rare."

I looked down. The news of Priscilla's great relationship with Mike's family stung. Mike's family had never approved of me, and I'd always consoled myself with the idea that Mike's parents wouldn't have gotten along with any of Mike's girlfriends. But I suppose I just wasn't to their taste, and that was more than a little hurtful.

"Anyway, it was good to see you, Chelsea," said Frank. "Hopefully next time we run into each other it will be under much happier circumstances. Like maybe we'll be at the zoo or something."

"Hold on one sec," I said. "I noticed Steven wasn't here either. What's up with that? He and Mike were inseparable back in the day."

Frank scoffed. "There's no way Steven would have shown up to something like this." His phone rang and he checked the caller ID. "I gotta get back to the city. It was good talking to you. Really."

Frank's car disappeared in a cloud of smoke. I struggled to see through the smoke but couldn't get a clear picture. Similarly, I couldn't form a clear picture of our investigation.

There was so much uncertainty, and I was having a hard time figuring out what move we should make next as fear mounted in my heart.

Still, despite the fear, a flame of determination flickered through my body. I knew I'd soon come across a piece of information that would break the case wide open. I just didn't know where I'd find that information, or if Miss May, Teeny, and I would be able to catch the killer before they struck again.

18

PIE PLEASE

*M*iss May yanked open the farmhouse fridge with a vigorous tug. "Who wants apple pie?"

"Me! Oh! I do!" Teeny stretched her hand up like a grade-school kid. "Miss May!"

"Don't worry, Teeny. It was more of a rhetorical question," said Miss May. "I know we all want pie."

"Can I have sprinkles on mine?" Teeny asked.

"Absolutely not." Miss May set a pie tin on the counter and cut three big slices. "My apple pie is a pure creation. It can be combined with vanilla ice cream, whipped cream, or caramel. That's it."

"That's so mean." Teeny turned away and glowered.

I prepped a pot of decaf coffee, squatting down to eye-level to make sure enough water was in the reservoir. "Sounds like Teeny doesn't want any pie, Miss May. Can I have her slice?"

"You two are in such foul moods," said Teeny. "It's not my fault the memorial service was a bust."

"The service was far from a bust." Miss May selected a

fresh tub of hand-churned vanilla bean ice cream from the freezer.

"Was too! The only interesting part about it was the people who weren't there," Teeny said. "That's boring."

"Boring but helpful for the investigation," said Miss May. "We already checked Priscilla's alibi, so her absence doesn't indicate anything nefarious. But it seems very strange that Mike's friend Steven wasn't there. Chelsea, you said they were close."

"They were two peas in a business suit back in the day." I grabbed a spoon and dug into the carton of ice cream, pulling out a nice big bite for myself. "Where is this ice cream from? It's so thick."

Miss May plunged an ice creamer scooper into the carton with a smile. She'd warmed the scooper in hot water, so it cut through the vanilla bean with ease, creating a big, perfect ball of ice cream. "Got it from *The Cherry on Top* the other day. Traded Emily a Christmas tree for a month's worth of free ice cream."

"Don't tell KP," I said. "That's one more tree that went unsold."

Miss May warmed up the pie then added a big scoop of ice cream on top of each slice. Teeny and I grabbed our plates with greedy little smiles.

"Does this count as brain food?" I asked.

"Not sure," said Miss May. "Ask me again once we've talked more about the investigation."

The three of us settled at the kitchen table and ate our pie in silence for a few moments. Miss May hadn't changed anything about that kitchen in my entire life. The heavy, wooden cabinets were warm and homey. The tiled floor was scuffed up from years of foot traffic. The kitchen table still had a chunk taken out from that time I'd accidentally bashed it with a hammer.

The Japanese have a concept called *wabi sabi*, which they use to describe items or buildings that have extra character, added by years of use. They revere buildings that have a touch of peeling paint. Shoes with a scuff or two are considered beautiful. People, even, are loved for their wrinkles and imperfections.

Miss May's kitchen (and the entire farm, actually) had tons of wabi sabi. All the signs of wear helped me feel at home. And I liked to think about the wabi sabi that comes with being human, too. None of us are perfect, and that's what makes everyone special.

Teeny finished her apple pie fastest, sitting back with a dazed, sugar-induced smile. "That was good. Barely missed the sprinkles."

I looked down at my plate. I hadn't taken more than two or three bites of the pie, yet Teeny's plate had been literally licked clean.

"We need to enter you in some kind of eating contest," I said. "You inhaled that pie like an American champion."

"If Miss May's pie is being served, I'll enter any eating contest you can find," said Teeny. "Also happy to enter a contest where the only food being consumed is sprinkles. Finally, I just want to say that I'm open to catering an eating contest, if you either of you have any connections in the competitive eating world."

"Why would we have connections in the competitive eating world?" said Miss May.

Teeny shrugged. "Chelsea lived in Manhattan for a few years. She has all kinds of fancy friends."

"Competitive eaters are not fancy people," said Miss May.

"Whatever." Teeny jumped up and headed over to the kitchen island. "Can I have the last slice or what?"

"There's half a pie left," said Miss May, laughing. "Take whatever you want."

Teeny cut a huge slice and tossed it in the microwave. "The way I see it, we're gonna need to track down the missing best friend, Steve-o."

"Steven," I said.

Teeny nodded. "Best friendships can turn sour faster than I can finish a slice of pie. And what did you say Frank said about the guy, Chelsea?"

"He said Steven would have never gone to something like a memorial service," I said. "And then he just disappeared. It was so weird."

"Is it possible this Frank fella is a suspect?" said Miss May.

I shrugged. "Hard to say. But I think we'd be better off focusing on Steven. The two of them were so, so close back in the day. I don't care what anybody says, the fact that he didn't show up for the memorial is weird."

"What about Mike's ex?" Miss May turned to me. "Jenny was her name?"

"Frank says she and Mike were good," I said.

"But didn't you say Mike called her 'Jealous Jenny?'" said Teeny.

I nodded. "Yeah. But who knows what that could have meant, coming from Mike. Besides, if the girl was so jealous, she would have killed Priscilla, not Mike, right?"

"So, we're back to the missing best friend and business partner," said Teeny. "How close were they back in the day? Really?"

"Mike and Steven were always together," I said. "But they fought a lot, too. Bickered like an old married couple."

"Like I said," said Teeny. "Best friends can turn murderous so fast it'll make your head fall off."

"You know, Teeny, as your best friend, this is a little disconcerting," said Miss May. "Do you think our friendship could turn murderous like that?"

"Absolutely," said Teeny. "You keep denying me sprinkles for my pie, there's no telling how violent I might get. And I don't know if you've noticed, but it's not like I'm getting any *less* annoying. Decent chance one day you'll snap. Look up. There's blood on your hands. You're all like 'what have I done,' then it comes to you in a flash. The anger. The rage. The memory of the horrible thing you've done. Then you head for Saudi Arabia and spend your retirement as a date farmer in a small village, bonding with the locals."

Miss May furrowed her brows. "Why Saudi Arabia?"

Teeny popped her pie out of the microwave. "No extradition."

"Why do you know which countries have no extradition?" I asked.

"You're the one suspected of murder," said Teeny. "Why do you not?"

"I'm not even going to justify that with a response," I said. "Have we agreed to question Mike's friend Steven next or what?"

We all agreed. Then I ate a second slice of pie. Then I ate a third slice (just a sliver!). Then I went to bed.

19

SUGAR SUGAR

*T*hat night, I struggled to fall asleep, which was not new for me. But it was too cold to go out and visit See-Saw. I knew my sleep troubles had been caused by eating a ton of rich, sugary pie right before bed. I decided to wait for a sugar crash, reasoning that I'd be hit by a wave of exhaustion as soon as the sugar worked its way through my system.

The crash must have come, because one second, I was lying awake, counting sheep, and what felt like the next, I jolted awake with my heart pounding in my chest. The remnants of a nightmare took up residence in my throat, sending a wave of anxiety through my entire body.

In the nightmare, Mike and I were together again. We were standing in the living room of our New York apartment, arguing. The first terrifying detail: both Mike and I were wearing wedding rings in the nightmare, and the walls were decorated with photos from our wedding day. But those weren't the only off-kilter details about what I'd dreamt. The entire room was suffused with a burnt orange glow. A litter of angry cats yowled and cried, crisscrossing at our feet every few seconds. Mike's *Goldfinger* poster was four times larger than it is in real life. It had been removed from the wall and rested beside a large wall safe which was propped open one or two inches.

Mike and I were arguing about the safe. I kept moving toward it as we bickered back and forth, but whenever I took a step, he'd step closer, blocking my path.

"Just let me see inside," I said. "We're married. What could you possibly have to hide from me?"

"Married people are allowed to have privacy, Chelsea. That's healthy."

"Are you seriously claiming that it's healthy for you to have a massive safe in our living room and not tell me what's inside? Mike. That's so messed up."

"Here you go with the name calling!"

"I didn't say *you're* messed up. I said it's messed up for you to hide whatever is in that safe from me."

The ethereal orange glow intensified as the argument got more heated. So, too, did the chaotic yowls of the unhappy cats.

"You adopted ninety-seven unhappy cats, and you don't see me complaining about it," said Mike.

"I didn't adopt them! They came in through the window. What do you want me to do? Kick them out? They're cats, Mike. They need us. They need us."

"OK, fine," said Mike. "That's the difference between these two situations then. The cats need us. But under no circumstances do you need to know what's in that safe."

"What are you hiding?" Tears streamed down my cheeks.

Mike's voice turned cold and hard. "There are things, Chelsea, that are best left untouched. Some secrets must remain buried."

I stammered in disbelief, unable to accept his evasive response. The yearning to uncover the truth clawed at my throat. I stepped forward, my voice trembling with a mix of defiance and vulnerability. "We promised each other complete honesty when we got married."

A moment of hesitation flickered in Mike's eyes, but then he closed the safe with a resounding, metallic thud, cutting off my access to its mysterious contents. The sound of the clanking metal reverberated throughout the room. Suddenly the cats were gone. I reached out to touch the cold surface of the safe, but it slipped away like smoke, dissolving into nothingness.

And then I woke, my fingers still tingling with the fear and anger I'd felt in the nightmare world. The dream had left me disoriented and unsure. I had a vague memory of arguing with Mike about the safe. But how much had come from the nightmare world, and how much had really happened?

Most importantly: what had Mike been keeping in that safe?

The safe symbolized all the secrets Mike might have kept from me and others. Yet as I lay there, I knew there was more to the dream than mere symbolism. It was as if my subconscious was desperately trying to communicate a message, urging me to delve deeper into this case, and into the truth of what had lain hidden in that safe.

I glanced around the room, half expecting to have been transported back to the bedroom I'd shared with Mike in the city. Shadows from the tree limbs outside danced on the walls, creating an eerie ambience all around me. Fear began to creep back into my body, then Steve the dog nudged me with his nose and brought me back to the present.

Just like that, my fear turned to determination. I knew

beyond all doubt that Teeny, Miss May, and I would solve the mystery of the safe, and catch Mike's killer. I owed it to myself to solve the mystery, and to finally get some closure on my botched relationship with Mike.

Taking a deep breath, I swung my legs out of the bed. A newfound resolve burned within me. The journey ahead was uncertain and fraught with potential for the pain of new and old wounds alike. But I would not allow myself to be haunted by mutated memories of the past.

And I would do my best to avoid eating tons of sugar right before bed.

20

HONKING GOOD TIME

*T*he sound of honking horns woke me the next morning. I rubbed my eyes and rolled over. Steve the dog was looking at me like, "What's with all the ruckus?"

"I've got no clue. Let's just hope it's got nothing to do with dead bodies."

Steve made a throaty little guttural sound, somewhere between a groan and a whine. He wanted breakfast. And he wanted to be let out. And he wanted to know why I'd woken up sweaty and terrified in the middle of the night.

I explained the nightmare as I got dressed for the day, keeping only to the most pertinent details. By the time I'd pulled on my jeans and my college sweatshirt, Steve was running back and forth at my feet, wagging his tail like a metronome.

He bounded down the steps at my side, then darted straight over to his Snuffy Mat over by the kitchen door. For all you cat lovers out there, a Snuffy Mat is kind of like a patch of shag carpet you can use to serve a hungry dog his or her dry food in. The mat recreates the look and feel of scavenging for food out in the forest, so it keeps your pup's brain occupied. Plus, it slows down their eating, which is a good thing for Steve, because if he isn't slowed down, he'll eat so fast it'll make him puke.

I tossed some food in the mat, then stepped outside to see what was up with all the honking. A line of cars trailed all the way down the entrance to the driveway and out into the road. KP walked up and down the line, handing little pieces of paper to the driver of each car, and greeting them with a smile.

"Bet you're wondering what's going on?"

I turned to see Miss May all dressed for the day, wearing jeans and her red flannel coat with a matching hat.

"You gonna tell me?"

"Only if you tell me about your bad dream first."

"How do you know about that?" I covered my mouth and widened my eyes. "Oh no. Did I wake up screaming or something?"

"Nah. You haven't screamed from a nightmare since you were at least twenty-nine. I heard you telling Steve all about it, though. Sounds like your subconscious was pulling you back toward that safe."

"I guess so... I can't shake the feeling that whatever Mike was keeping in there is at the bottom of this murder." I headed inside to pour a cup of coffee. Miss May followed me. "It would make sense, wouldn't it? Safe is empty. Owner of the safe is dead."

Miss May nodded. "The murder and the robbery certainly seem connected." She winced as more honks came from outside.

"You wanna tell me what this is all about now?" I said.

Miss May handed me a flier. There was an image of a lopsided Christmas tree in the middle and the text read:

KP'S UGLY CHRISTMAS TREE EXTRAVAGANZA

FIND AN UGLY TREE, GET IT FOR HALF OFF

I chuckled. "KP really wants to sell extra tress this year." A quick look outside revealed even more cars streaming out toward the road. "But are all these people here for ugly trees?"

"Apparently KP has been working quite closely with our new social media guru," said Miss May.

I lunged forward. "Eduardo? I haven't seen him step foot on this farm in at least a year!"

"He 'works remotely,'" said Miss May. "I guess Eduardo found out that ugly Christmas trees were trending online. He tried to contact us, but we were investigating. Then he got a hold of KP, and now we're here."

I laughed. "This is kind of awesome. But we better go help out."

Miss May clinked her coffee mug with mine. "Let's do it."

The first person I ran into out by the Christmas trees was none other than Pine Grove's own Chief Flanagan. Flanagan, typically runway ready and more glamorous than anyone in town, was wearing rumpled jeans and a stained sweatshirt. Her hair looked unwashed, and her eyes were bloodshot.

"Chief Flanagan, hi." I approached her like I might approach a raccoon that was out during the day. "Can I help you?"

"Chelsea. Yes! Yes, I think you can." She swallowed hard and stared at me with those bloodshot eyes. I waited for her to say more, but no further words arrived.

"What can I do for you?" I said.

"Right! Right. Wow, I'm sorry. I've been so scattered lately. Have I ever told you how beautiful your eyes are?"

"You've told me how much I don't deserve Wayne a few times. But I'm not sure you've ever mentioned how you feel about my eyes." Snarky, I know. But Flanagan had been so tough on me over the years. Even though she was clearly in distress, could anyone really expect me to drop my drama at the door?

"You're right, Chelsea. I've been tough on you. And I'm sorry about all that. It's just, this guy, Commissioner Tate? He has been riding me like a coin-operated bull at a North Carolina dive bar. I think I've been wound up tight because of it, saying and doing things that are not like me at all." She leaned forward. "Tate docked my pay every time an amateur sleuth solved a murder before me. It's happened so many times... I'm getting very little in terms of compensation these days."

"That's totally unfair," I said, feeling sympathy for Flanagan for one of the first times ever.

"It is what it is," said Flanagan, breathless. "His bureaucracy tied my hands on every investigation, then he penalized me for not getting things done. That's why I'm doing things my own way now. That's why you're not in jail for murdering Michael Gherkin." Flanagan's casual reference to my potential jail time formed a lump in my throat. She kept talking before I had a chance to issue a response. "Anyway, I know this is unorthodox, but I need to return my Christmas tree."

I stammered. We'd never had a return before. Again, acting before I had a chance to respond, Flanagan charged from the grove over to the parking lot, where a Christmas tree was strapped to the topof her car.

"It's as good as new. See?" She reached out to touch it. Dozens of dry bristles cascaded off the branch she'd touched. "OK. Maybe it's a little dry. But I don't think I'm going to be here for Christmas. I just don't need it."

"When did we sell this to you?" I asked.

"November thirtieth," said Flanagan, without missing a beat.

"And you haven't taken it off your car this whole time?"

"With the Commissioner, and the murders, and everything else going on... I haven't had the time."

Flanagan's voice wavered as she referenced 'everything else going on'. In that moment, I saw through her tough exterior, and she suddenly looked like a little girl to me. Big, innocent eyes. A hard determination that rose from necessity from a young age. A wisdom behind it all that must have existed since her first day in kindergarten.

"Are you OK?" I said.

"I'm fine." The way she spoke made it clear she wouldn't be going into further details that day. That was alright with me, as I had bigger problems to worry about.

I agreed to take the tree back, mostly because I was excited to tell KP he had to sell one more tree in order to break even with last year. But I also agreed to accept Flanagan's unorthodox return because I could tell there was something going seriously wrong in her life.

I'd held a grudge against Mike for almost every single day after he left me at the altar. Now he was dead, and I'd never have a chance to repair things with him. Flanagan had been crummy to me, that was for sure. But it seemed I had a chance to patch things up with her, and I wasn't going to let myself miss that opportunity.

I made a mental note to clear the air with Flanagan after Mike's killer was behind bars. I wanted to befriend her, sure. But I also wanted to solve the mystery of what was going on in her life. Because people rarely change in small towns, and when they do, it's almost always for a reason.

21

UGLY CHRISTMAS

*B*y the time afternoon rolled around, we'd sold every single one of our less fortunate looking Christmas trees and put out a sign to turn new customers away. KP lounged in the bakeshop, munching on an apple cider donut and laughing to himself.

"I'm a marketing genius, that's what I am," he said. "Should have gone and worked in advertising like one of those furious men."

"Do you mean 'mad men?'" I asked.

"Quit knowing everything," said KP, investigating the donut like the next bite he took would be the most important bite in the world. "Don't you get tired of that ever?"

"She must," said Miss May, wiping down the glass pastry case. "Can you imagine how exhausting it would be to know every single fact in the world and be unable to keep that knowledge to yourself, no matter the circumstances?"

"I'm not that bad," I said. "And yes, as a matter of fact, it can be exhausting."

The doors to the bakeshop crashed open and Teeny

entered with a huge smile. "Greetings earthlings and Chelsea!"

"What are you in such a good mood for?" said Miss May.

"I'm happy for you. Folks down at the restaurant are talking like you've sold out of uggo trees." She pointed at KP. "You, sir, are a marketing genius. Like one of those 'angry men' working down on Madison Avenue in the city."

KP and Miss May both turned to me, waiting for me to correct Teeny. I shoved a whole donut in my mouth to keep myself from saying anything. Everyone laughed, except for Teeny, who planted her fists on her hips in annoyance.

Teeny demanded to be let in in the joke, but Miss May waved her off. "It was nothing, seriously. And we don't have time to talk about mad men, anyhow. We need to discuss how we're going to find this Steven guy."

"Chelsea knows everything," said Teeny. "I bet she can lead us right to him."

"I have a pretty good idea where he is," I said, grinning sheepishly. "But that's not because I know everything. It's because I've been there before. And I have an exceptional memory." Teeny rolled her eyes. I grabbed my keys and dangled them in front of her face, smiling. "Ready to go?"

Steven grew up on one of the nicest streets in Blue Mountain. Huge oak trees were lined up on either side of the street, with equal distance from one tree to the next. Beautiful, black streetlamps were stationed on every corner. A pair of teenage boys played basketball on a hoop that had been set up on the side of the road.

The kids stopped playing and stepped aside as we drove past. They both had thick, dark eyebrows and mischievous grins. For some reason, their energy gave me an uneasy feeling. Once Steven's parents' place came into view, that uneasy feeling multiplied.

"I haven't been to this place in over ten years," I said as a shiver worked its way down my arms and legs.

"What makes you think Steven still lives here?" Miss May asked.

"He was one of those guys," I said. "Never used to shut up about how much he loved living at home, saving money and eating his mom's home cooked meals.Mike was always trying to convince the guy to move down to the city, but he simply refused."

"Man after my own heart," said Teeny. "Men were always trying to get me to move to the city back in the day."

"But you never went?" I asked.

"I went for my first two husbands. But every husband after that I said 'I'm staying here. Take it or leave it.'"

"And they almost always left it," said Miss May.

"No problem with me." Teeny looked me square in the eye. "If a man ever asks you to choose between living around family and moving somewhere new, he's not a keeper. Trust me, I know."

Steven was outside his parents' house when we pulled up, chiseling at black ice with a long, skinny stick. He stopped working as I climbed out of the car and headed toward him. I waved but he did not wave back.

"Long time, no Steve," I said, giving him a big, open smile. The guy didn't return my smile. I continued as though he had. "You look good."

"Feel terrible," said Steve. "I don't know if you heard, but—"

"I found the body," I said, pivoting to a much more serious tone of voice. "I'm really sorry about what happened."

He grabbed the ice pick tight. I noticed a long, metal spike protruding off the end. I swallowed.

"Hey, uh, any chance you could maybe talk for a few?" I said.

"I think I can take a break from this world-changing work I'm doing," said Steve. "But not for long. The fate of the universe hangs in the balance."

I'd forgotten how sardonic Steve could be. His sarcasm made him a difficult communicator . But I resolved to keep as sunny and upbeat an attitude as I could. Steven nodded politely as I introduced Teeny and Miss May. All the while, he kept his hand wrapped around that ice pick. Once the introductions were over, he ran his tongue over his teeth and gave me the up and down.

"So, you think I killed Gherkin, I take it?"

"What? No! No, no, no..." I was not a good liar. Steven seemed all-too aware of that.

"Hey, I don't blame you," he said. "You dated Mike for so long. I'm sure he told you what he did to me."

My quick glance at Miss May must have revealed how little I knew about what Steven was talking about. He clocked it and then tossed his head back, laughing. "Wow. Wow! Mike never told you. The three of us were hanging out all the time, but he still managed to keep it a secret from you. Man, that guy was pathological."

"What did he not tell me?" I asked.

"He never told you why I live with my parents, or why I never went to get my business degree like the rest of the guys," said Steven.

I shook my head. He jammed the ice pick into a new patch. I jumped back and coughed loudly, trying to cover my fear. The guy knew how to apply force with that ice pick, and he didn't seem like the kind of person who would back out of confrontation. In a flash, I imagined him bludgeoning Mike over the head with a rock or a paperweight, then looting the safe and running out of Mike's place. I knew better than to draw conclusions, but the guy was such a live wire, it was hard to keep a measured mind about him.

"Your little boyfriend cheated off me in b-school," said Steven, applying the world's cringiest abbreviation for business school. "Sat next to me for a whole semester in stats. Took every answer off every one of my tests. End of the semester, they got suspicious, figured the whole thing out."

I couldn't help but to step back and blink a few times in confusion. The news flabbergasted me. Though on many levels it also made perfect sense. "I guess, when I think about it, I'm not surprised."

"None of us are," said Miss May, taking a step toward Steven. "But weren't you friends with him right up 'til his almost-wedding to Chelsea? I remember seeing you at the church that day."

"I had a rough childhood. Didn't want to believe my buddy would pull something like that with me. Then, when he left Chelsea standing at the altar like that, I knew. Gherkin had more hair than he did morals, and the guy had a very poor head of hair."

"Cheating is messed up," I said. "But why were you so angry about it? Why are you so angry about it now?"

"I got kicked out of b-school, Chelsea!" Steven jammed the ice pick into the frozen ground, and it stood at attention. "Mike didn't get in a single ounce of trouble. His parents pulled strings like their precious lives depended on it. But life after that, for me? Look around! I'm still sleeping in my rocket-ship bed."

"I'm so sorry that happened," said Miss May.

"Me too," said Teeny. "Cheaters never quit, and quitters never win."

"That's not a saying," I whispered to Teeny.

She cleared her throat and spoke loudly. "My apologies. I've been informed that the expression I just used is not a 'real' expression. Thank you so much, Chelsea, for keeping me in line."

Steven looked down and let out a small laugh. "You ladies have a lot of quirk. You know that?"

"We also have a job to do," said Miss May. "Can you tell us where you were the night that Michael Gherkin was killed?"

"You're seriously here to accuse me, huh?" Steven looked away and laughed. "You know what? No. I'm not here for it."

"But –" I began.

"I said no, OK?" said Steven. "How dare you show up at my mom's house and accuse me of murder. Leave now, or I'll call the cops and report you for trespassing, and for harassment, and for being bad dressers."

"Whoa," said Teeny. "Trespassing and harassment, I can allow. But we look very cute today!"

"I'm wearing my best flannel," said Miss May.

Steven pulled his phone out of his pocket. "Are you going or not?"

GRILLED MYSTERIES

*S*teven lived near our favorite burger shack in town, *Ewing's Eats*, so we headed over there to debrief after leaving his place. The owner of the spot, Patrick Ewing, greeted us with a squinting smile.

"Don't tell me. You think I killed somebody, and you want one last Ewing burger before you bring me in to the police station."

Miss May chuckled. "You got it, Patrick."

He held eye contact with her for a long moment. "How you doing, May? How are things with the grave digger?"

"John is the head of parks and rec for the town of Pine Grove," said Miss May, referencing her love interest, John Wentworth. "And we're both doing well, thank you."

"They're a very cute couple," said Teeny.

"Yeah, yeah, yeah." Patrick rolled his eyes and handed a few menus out through the pass-thru.

The truth was, Miss May and John Wentworth were one of the cutest new couples in Pine Grove, but they'd struggled to find time to enjoy each other's company. John's work kept him busy all day, every day, and Miss May often went to sleep early in order to wake up and handle farm work in the mornings.

I'm not going to say they were on the rocks. But I knew that John was going to need to find a way to make time for Miss May. There were plenty of suitors in Pine Grove, including Patrick Ewing, and I suspected they were all secretly waiting in the wings to sweep her off her feet.

We ordered burgers and fries, then settled in at a picnic table under an industrial sized heat lamp.

"What are we thinking about Mike's friend, Steven?" said Miss May, handing out napkins and utensils.

"He's the killer," said Teeny. "Isn't that obvious?"

"Why do you say that?" said Miss May.

"He told us that Mike got him kicked out of business school. He blames Mike for ruining his life. Now Mike is dead." Teeny sipped soda from a Styrofoam cup. "Basically handed us the murder weapon, wrapped in cute Christmas paper. I figured we were going to pound some burgers, build up our strength, go back and force him down to the station."

"When we find the killer, we don't usually stop for burgers before taking them down," I said.

Teeny shrugged. "First time for everything."

"I don't think Steven killed Mike," I said.

"You gotta be kidding me," said Teeny. "The guy handed us his motive on a silver platter!"

"Would you do that if you were the guilty party?" said Miss May. "He acted like he had nothing to hide. Told us everything about the cheating scandal without hesitation. Besides, those guys have been out of business school forever. Why would he have murdered Mike over such an ancient dispute?"

Patrick dropped a few trays of food at the table. "Pause

the murder talk, ladies. Your food has arrived." He winked at Miss May. "Tossed a few extra fries in yours."

Miss May looked away, face reddening, as Patrick sauntered back toward the burger shack.

"You better be careful, May," said Teeny. "Looks like the burger king is looking for a queen."

"He's just being a flirt," said Miss May, squirting ketchup onto her plate. "Chelsea, what do you think?"

"I think he wants you to be his burger queen," I said flatly.

"About Steven!" said Miss May.

"I think it's impossible to know for sure what's up with Steven," I said. "We need to keep learning more about him. And it might be smart to learn more about that cheating scandal too."

"Thoughts on how we can make that happen?" Miss May asked.

I was about to lay out a plan when Miss May handed me my little baggy of food. When I pulled out my grilled cheese, I started salivating immediately. Thick slices of sourdough were perfectly grilled, with a nice layer of brown crunch on top. Cheddar and American cheese spilled out the sides, oozing out and pooling on the sandwich wrapper. I took a bite, savoring the buttery crunch of the bread, then smiling as I got down to the layers of melted cheese.

"Oh... My goodness. This is the best Grilled Cheese I've ever had," I said. "How have I never gotten this here before?"

"I know. Patrick's food is incredible." Miss May popped a fry in her mouth with a smile.

"Can John Wentworth cook?" said Teeny, eyes dancing.

"Chelsea was about to tell us how we can get to the bottom of the cheating scandal," said Miss May. "I think that's far more important than a deep dive into John's skills in the kitchen."

Teeny winced. "He can't cook at all, can he?"

Miss May stammered. I jumped in to bail her out. "Mike used to use my laptop for a ton of his schoolwork when he was in business school. I'll do a search and find out who his stats professor was."

"Then what do we do?" said Miss May.

"We go down to NYU, and we see what the professor has to say about all this," I said. "Unless one of you has a better plan."

23

PROFESSING THE TRUTH

"   love the city around Christmas time," said Teeny, her forehead pressed against the back window of my car. "Everything is so romantic. Look at that beautiful couple, holding hands outside a little bar. And there's a young mother, getting her toddler all bundled up in a hat and gloves for a walk through Greenwich Village. And look over there! That nice young man is... Oh! Oh no! He's holding up a sign that says our president should take his ideas and shove them right up his –"

"We can all see the sign, Teeny," said Miss May. "Let's maybe focus more on the charm of the city, less on the signage."

We were just a few blocks north of the NYU campus. I'd been looking for parking for almost ten minutes with no luck, and with each moment my body tensed just a bit more. "I'm just going to pay to park in a garage," I said. "This is ridiculous. And if we don't get down to NYU soon, we're going to miss our chance to talk to Professor Green."

According to the search I'd conducted through my old emails, Mike and Steven had been students in Professor

Green's statistics course back in the day. As far as I could tell, the guys hadn't shared any other stats classes, so I felt confident Green was the right guy to talk to about the cheating scandal.

Green was speaking on an ethics panel that night, and it was his last school commitment before NYU went on winter break for nearly a month. The looming winter hiatus raised the stakes of our mission, and contributed greatly to my parking panic down in the village.

What if we missed our chance to speak to Green? What if he took off to Europe for a month to hob knob with other fancy professors? What if --

"Spot!" Teeny leaned between me and Miss May, pointing out the windshield. "See it!"

"There's a fire hydrant," said Miss May. "We've told you a dozen times, you can't park within a dozen feet of a fire hydrant in New York City."

"And I've told *you* a dozen times: that rule is stupid and there are never any fires in the winter anyway."

"That's preposterous, Teeny," said Miss May. "I'm willing to be there are more fires in New York City in winter months than in summer months. People run their heat more. They cook at home more. They use their fireplaces more. They cause fires more."

As Miss May and Teeny jumped into the deep end of their argument, I zeroed in on my parking problem, scanning both sides of the street for a spot. Within a few seconds, all the sounds of their argument dropped out. All I could hear were the sounds of cars on the street. Tires crunching over loose asphalt. Trucks beeping as they backed up. Then I saw a spot open up about ten feet ahead. I pressed the gas, hurrying toward it. We got closer, and closer, and closer.

Then, in what felt like the blink of an eye, we were standing in the lobby of NYU's Stern School of Business, and Professor Gary Green was walking toward us, deep in conversation with an orbital ring of eager students.

"Personal ethics and business ethics must be divested in order for true capitalism to thrive," said one young man.

"Disagree completely," said another. "Only through deepening the connection between personal and business ethics can capitalism continue to thrive as it has. We're no longer in the plundering age of the industrial revolutionists! The social responsibility of big business –"

"The social responsibility of big business is a passing fancy," said a young woman. "As the American people fall out of love with socially conscious spending, so too will our businesses relinquish the purported desire to 'help the world' through the products they sell, or how they sell them."

"But the American people's commitment to socially conscious spending isn't going anywhere," said the first man.

"It may seem that way now," said the young woman. "But market behavior has a direct relationship with consumer behavior. You watch and see. When our economy plummets, which it will, because those vacillations are part of any robust economy, the American consumer will suddenly be far less concerned with buying shoes from a company that also donates shoes to the homeless, and instead be focused solely on getting the best price on their own shoes."

"When did we start talking about shoes?" said Teeny, loud enough for the whole crew to stop and look at her. "And why do all of you talk with that funny accent? Like you're asking questions, but you're actually saying normal sentences."

Professor Green stepped forward. I recognized him from photos I'd seen online. Thick glasses. Condescending smile. A salt-n'-pepper beard that was trimmed to the perfect length. "I'm sorry. I don't think I saw you in the audience this evening. And you are…"

"We're friends of Steven Levine and Michael Gherkin," said Teeny. "Remember them?"

I blanched. On the way down we'd discussed being careful in our approach. It seemed Teeny, triggered perhaps by the obnoxious school chatter she'd witnessed, and eager to prove herself, had tossed that approach out the window for a far more aggressive angle. Miss May gave me a look like, "We should have seen that coming."

Green said hushed farewells to the students, promising them he'd catch up with them for drinks soon. Once they cleared the lobby, he turned back to us. "I don't have anything to say about Michael Gherkin or Steven Levine."

"If that were true, why did you ask your students to leave before talking to us?" said Miss May. "And why are your hands shoved so far into your pockets they're about to explode out the other side?"

"Perhaps I don't like being accosted by ignoramus' in the middle of a pleasant evening," said the man.

"I'm not an ignorant anus!" said Teeny. "How dare you!"

I cringed. "That is not what he called us."

"Well, I don't care!" Teeny puffed out her chest and stood tall. "You know, you college people all think you're so smart. Where are your street smarts though? Where's your ability to roll with the hunches?"

"Do you mean –" the professor began.

"No, I do not mean 'punches,'" said Teeny. "I'm a sleuth. I roll with the hunches. And I've got a hunch, right now, that you're lying through your yellow teeth."

"You may not be aware of this," said Miss May. "But Michael Gherkin was recently found dead, murdered in his own home. Steven Levine freely told us Gherkin was the reason Levine was kicked out of business school. If that's true –"

"No." Professor Green removed his hands from his pockets and smoothed out his sports coat. "I can't discuss this with you. I have to go. My students are waiting."

He pushed past us and exited out onto the city streets. I was ready to give up, go to dinner, and regroup. But Miss May followed the professor outside, zipping up her coat as she charged after him.

"Professor, wait!" she said.

He stopped walking. Turned around slowly. "I said I don't want to talk about this."

"You said you *can't* talk about this," said Miss May. "As a professor of business, I'm sure you realize the importance of language, no? Word choice, diction… It says a lot about our true intentions. In some cases, an entire contract could hinge on a single word, billions of dollars in the balance."

The professor scrubbed a hand over his face. "Who are you people?"

"My name is Mabel Thomas. I'm a former New York City prosecutor. Now I run an apple orchard and catch killers in my spare time. Well, I suppose I catch killers and run the orchard in my spare time. I believe there is no difference between business and personal ethics. Businesses are people in the eyes of the government, isn't that right? They have the same responsibilities we do."

"I was waiting for someone to make that point," said the professor.

"In the case of your murdered former student, Michael Gherkin, I believe you have an ethical responsibility to tell us if you know anything that might lead to the arrest of his killer," said Miss May. "We need to know what happened with that cheating scandal, and we need to know tonight."

A trio of police cars zoomed past us, sirens blaring. Teeny plugged her ears and closed her eyes. I kept my gaze settled on Professor Green. His face looked eerie, awash in the red and blue lights of the squad cars. Miss May, too, stayed focused on him. Once the sound had died down, she took a step toward him. "Why can't you talk to us about Steven Levine's expulsion?" said Miss May. "Tell us what you know."

24

COLD CASE, COLDER FRIES

"*L*et me get this straight." Wayne sipped his coffee. "According to this professor, Steven Levine was suing the school for wrongful expulsion?"

I nodded. Other than the fact that the two of us were discussing the violent murder of my evil ex, the scene was cozy as could be. It was pretty late, and we were the only customers left in the dining room at *Grandma's*. A half-eaten plate of French fries rested between us. Jazzy Christmas music floated toward us from ceiling-mounted speakers. Every so often Petey pushed an old-fashioned vacuum cleaner past, and the place smelled faintly of the cleaning solution he'd used on every table but ours.

"That's right." I grabbed a cold fry and popped it in my mouth. No, the fry didn't taste great. But it was a fried potato. What was I supposed to do? Leave it there to die? "And Levine is just a month or two out from getting a multi-million dollar payout."

"Why did the professor tell you all this?"

"He resisted quite a bit," I said. "But then Miss May came

at him with big time prosecutor energy, and he crumbled like a Christmas cookie on Groundhog's Day."

"There's nothing wrong with a six-week-old crumbly cookie," said Wayne.

"You know I agree with you there," I said.

Petey parked his vacuum beside our table and squatted down beside us. "Hey you two. Just wanted to let you know, if you were any other customers, I'd be asking you to leave right now. But you're Chelsea and Wayne, so instead I'm just going to ask you to lock up when you leave. Maybe scrape your plate and leave it in the sink before you go?"

I smiled. Only in the world's cutest small towns (run by the world's cutest little blonde ladies) are diners trusted to lock up for the night. Sure, Teeny was like family to me. But the gesture warmed my heart.

"Oh. And Teeny has a message for you personally, Detective Hudson," said Petey.

Wayne arched his eyebrows, displaying curiosity. Petey cleared his throat and read a text off his phone. "Dear Officer Beef Boy, I will be personally insulted if you try to pay for those fries. Don't leave money in the cash register. Don't leave it on the table. I'm telling you, you big can of beef... If you pay, there will be trouble in the morning." Petey looked up at us with big, wide eyes. "Sorry for calling you beef. She said I had to read it word for word."

Petey hurried away as Wayne shook his head, laughing. "Teeny is very intense. Have you ever told her that?"

"If I ever went a day without telling her that, she'd be insulted," I said.

He ate a fry off the plate. *That's my guy, everyone! Just as likely to eat gross old fries as me. No wonder we love each other so much.* "So Steven Levine is about to get a big pay day, and it's been years since the cheating scandal. Why risk it all for revenge after fighting through such a long legal case?"

"Exactly. This is why I'm not convinced Levine killed Mike."

"Are you thinking the professor could have killed Mike? Maybe Mike testified on behalf of Levine. Maybe he somehow implicated the professor in the scandal. Is it possible the professor is about to lose his job over this?"

"He's scheduled to teach three classes next semester, so I doubt it," I said. "You should have seen the guy. He's beloved. It's like he's King of the Snobs down there. I don't think he'd ever risk that, especially not to help someone like Mike get ahead."

I watched as Petey left the restaurant. Standing, I grabbed the plate of fries and held it out to Wayne. "You want these?"

He grabbed a few, then I rescued the remainders and headed toward the back to clean the plate and stack it with the others. As soon as I entered the kitchen, I remembered why Petey was Teeny's favorite waiter. The kitchen was spotless. Pots and pans hung glistening from a wire rack. Stainless steel surfaces shimmered brighter than they did the day they were installed.

Wayne followed me in, took the plate from me and washed it off in the sink. "Now that Levine is out of the picture, who are you going to question next? Friends? Family? Didn't you say one of Mike's exes was at the memorial? Any chance she was at the service to gloat after a successful killing spree?"

"You need to kill more than one person to qualify for a spree," I said. "And Mike's friend, Frank, said that Mike and Jenny had patched things up anyway."

Wayne handed me the plate. "Who else hated Mike and would have wanted to frame you?"

I grabbed a rag and dried the plate off, stacking it on top of dozens of others just like it. The stack of dishes wobbled a bit as I added the newly cleaned dish to the pile. I reached out and steadied it, careful to set things right again. After a moment, a pang of frustration rippled through my body. Each of those plates nestled inside the next perfectly, creating a logical stack that was easy to steady. I knew, if I could only follow the right clues, they'd stack just as neatly. But I felt so far from the truth, almost like I'd never help bring justice back to Pine Grove.

"Chelsea?" Wayne put his hand on the small of my back. "You alright?"

I blinked. "Yeah. Um. I'm fine."

"We've gotta figure this out, or Flanagan is bound to turn her attention to you. I mean... You had motive, with Mike's wedding coming up. And that note..."

"You don't need to remind me of simple facts." My tone was sharper than I'd intended.

"I'm not trying to make you mad here. I'm just saying."

"I'm sorry," I said. "I know."

"You said Priscilla wasn't at the memorial either, right?" said Wayne. "She's got an alibi. And she hates your guts. But maybe if you track her down and sweet talk her, she'd be willing to help you, for Mike's sake."

I looked at the stack of plates, taunting me with their glimmering perfection. A sigh slipped from my lips. "You're probably right, Beef Boy. You're probably right."

25

DINER DISASTER

"According to the almighty Internet, Priscilla is a chef at a place called *Elmo's Diner* in Tarrytown, New York." I set my laptop on the kitchen table and Miss May crowded around it.

"That's her picture alright." Miss May put on her glasses and leaned forward. "I just can't believe that woman is a chef."

"Why?"

"Because she didn't seem like a chef," said Miss May, pulling a tray of Christmas cookies from the oven.

"I knew I smelled cookies," I said.

"Have one."

"I'm getting married on Christmas! If you keep feeding me cookies for breakfast like this, I'm going to plump right out of my wedding dress."

"Never heard the word 'plump' used quite that way before," said Miss May. "And that's fine. If you don't want a cookie..."

"You know I want one."

She smiled and extended the tray toward me. There

before me lay six rows of picture-perfect Christmas sugar cookies. Some were shaped like Santa, others like reindeer or candy canes. I leaned down and smelled them. Warm and buttery, just like I remembered from childhood.

"They smell incredible," I said, selecting a Santa cookie from the tray. "My mouth is literally watering."

Miss May set the tray down on a trivet and grabbed a candy cane cookie for herself. "Fresh-baked Christmas cookies on a cold winter morning are hard to beat." She smiled. "Remember how we used to do this when you had sick days from school? It didn't matter what season it was—"

"I would beg you to make Christmas cookies with me, and you always would." I smiled fondly at the memory. "I'm lucky you took me in after what happened."

"I'm lucky, too," said Miss May. "Now let's talk plans for today. Seems to me you and Wayne are right. We need to visit Priscilla. Is her restaurant open today?"

I clicked around on the restaurant's website. "Why do places make their hours so hard to find?"

"Go to Google reviews, they usually have them posted there," Miss May said.

"I don't need Internet help from my elderly aunt," I said, still clicking around blindly. "Fine. Come show me."

Miss May snickered, nudged me out of the way, and pulled up the hours of Priscilla's diner in two seconds flat. "I may be elderly, but I've got a ton of practice looking up restaurants online. It's basically my only hobby."

"You mean other than baking. And taking care of animals. And reading. And cooking. And –"

"Those aren't hobbies, they're just things that I do." Miss May snapped the laptop shut. "How's the cookie, anyway?"

I took my second bite. It broke off into my mouth without a sound. For a moment, I just let the cookie sit on my tongue. The taste exploded when I began to chew. It was so fluffy, it almost tasted like a slice of pillowy bread. I closed my eyes and savored every morsel.

"Oh good," said Miss May. "You like it."

We arrived at *Grandma's* a little while later to find Teeny outside waiting for us. She was wearing a puke-green sweater with rusty bells sloppily affixed to the front. I wrinkled my nose as she climbed into the T-bird.

"What's that sweater, Teeny? It looks like a junkyard and a landfill had a baby."

"I don't want to talk about it." Teeny sounded annoyed as she turned away and looked out the window.

Miss May and I exchanged a confused and somewhat delighted grin.

"You gotta talk about it now," said Miss May. "What happened? Did you get ripped off by another online ad?"

"No! I made this!" Teeny snorted a puff of air out her nose.

"Why?" I asked. "I mean, that sweater, it's… It's… It's…"

"It's really, extremely, terribly, horribly, hideously ugly?" said Teeny.

I shrugged. I didn't want to say it, but…

"Petey and the staff organized this event where we all wear 'ugly Christmas sweaters' to work today. I showed up and they were all wearing the cutest sweaters you've ever seen. Petey's has a funny looking elf on it with googly eyes. One of the cooks has one where baby Yoda is dressed like Santa Claus. I'm the only one who showed up with an actual ugly sweater! Now they're all pointing at me, snickering, 'cuz my sweater is actually, seriously, horribly, terribly ugly."

Miss May and I burst out laughing.

"Quit laughing at me!" Teeny crossed her arms and pouted. "I was just trying to play along."

"But Teeny!" Miss May slapped her knee. "Ugly Christmas sweaters are a global phenomenon. And they're not a new thing, either. Everyone knows they're not actually ugly. They're just silly and maybe a little...over-stated."

"I guess I'm just an old lady who can't keep up with the times."

"It's impressive that you made that yourself," I said, holding back a laugh. "Even if it does look like a sewage accident."

"Stop picking on me!" Teeny's angry shell collapsed into a big laugh of surrender. "Do you know how long it took me to find such an ugly color thread? I had to special order this stuff!"

We kept right on laughing as we drove down to Tarry-town. Teeny did all she could to defend her 'ugly Christmas sweater' misunderstanding. But the more she protested, the more we all laughed. Then she begged us to go to the mall so she could buy something new to put on, and we laughed even more.

It took almost an hour to get down to *Elmo's*, but it felt like no time at all, thanks to Teeny's antics. The restaurant was in a free-standing brick building down near the Hudson River. There was a green awning near the front door, and a hand-painted sign on the front window boasted "The Best Pancakes in Town."

We entered the restaurant through a vestibule that had been plastered with fliers for local music, art, and poetry performances. The inside of the restaurant teemed with cozy, yet alternative, charm. Framed images on the walls showed rock stars from the ages. Hip young couples ate at a long diner counter. Children's drawings of cute little ducks were tacked up behind the cash register, each one more chaotic than the last.

"This must be one of those 'cool' diners," said Teeny conspiratorially.

"Like yours?" I asked.

Teeny shook her head. "Mine is cool in a charming, small-town way. This one is cool in an alternative way. I bet half the servers have tattoos." As if on cue, a tattooed waitress bustled past us, carrying a tray of food. "See! Tatties everywhere."

"No one calls them 'tatties', Teeny," said Miss May.

A second tattooed waitress approached us. 50s. Brunette. "Y'all dining in?"

"Actually, we're just here to chat with Priscilla," said Miss May with a polite smile. "Is she in?"

Before we had a chance to reply, a huge bald man exploded out of the kitchen and into the dining room. His face was red, he had a small diamond earring, and he was wearing all black. "Tell me where she is, or I'm going to make a scene!"

A 20-something African American chef followed the bald guy out. He was much, much calmer than the bald man. "Zeke. As I've already said, no one here has seen her for days."

"Why are you even open then!?" said Zeke. "She's the head chef at this place. You can't keep *Elmo's* running without her."

"Of course, we can," said the chef. "We've all been trained. We know what we're doing."

Teeny nudged me hard in the ribs. "They're talking about Priscilla."

I was too focused on the argument between this 'Zeke' guy and the cook to respond, or to look in Teeny's direction.

"Tell me where she is." Zeke was no longer yelling. But the effort of speaking quietly had made a vein in his neck bulge. "I've gone to her house. I've come here two days in a row. Where is my sister? I know you know! She loved this place. She must be calling and checking in!"

The cook took a deep breath, then exhaled. "I can't keep repeating myself, man."

Zeke let out an angry, primal yelp. The next second, he spun on his heels and charged toward us with clenched fists. I could smell his overpowering tobacco and oak scented cologne as he pushed past me and stormed outside.

Once the angry man was gone, the cook made a public apology to the diners and offered everyone free biscuits on the house. The diners muttered their acceptance. An uneasy pall hung in the air.

I turned to Miss May. "Who was that guy?"

"Sounds like he's Priscilla's brother," she said. "We can't let him get away."

26

BURNING RUBBER

*H*igh speed car chases weren't new to me. You solve enough mysteries, you're bound to give chase a time or two. High speed car chase while driving my new T-bird, however, was a whole new story.

I peeled out of the *Elmo's* parking lot with screeching tires. The car fish-tailed and then straightened out, like a hose that I'd just gotten a firm grip on. I wanted to go fast, but I quickly realized I had no idea which car I was following.

"That way!" Miss May pointed after a red Corvette. "That's him!"

"Looks like it's about to be muscle car mayhem," said Teeny, shoving her head up between us. "Hope you're ready to gun it, Chels."

I took a beat to steady myself, made sure the coast was clear, then slammed down on the pedal with my dusty old Converse. Whatever Big Dan did to fix that car, I think he might have done it too well. The impact of my speed pressed my body back against the seat and widened my eyes to twice their normal size.

"Slow down!" said Miss May.

"Speed up!" said Teeny. "He's gonna get away!"

Without warning, the Corvette careened across three lanes and made a sharp turn onto a highway that followed the Hudson River south toward New York City. I had twenty feet to pull the same maneuver which, on a typical day, I would have needed at least two to three minutes to execute.

"Hang on, ladies!" I checked my rear view. A truck was barreling down the lane to my right, blocking my path to the riverside highway. The exit for the highway was getting closer and closer. "Here we go!"

I swerved. The truck driver honked his horn for ten seconds straight. Teeny cheered. Whoosh! Just like that, I'd made it four lanes over and was following the Corvette onto the highway.

"Oh yeah, mama! You nailed that move!" Teeny pumped her fist in the air.

"Please don't do that again," said Miss May, letting out a deep breath. "My life flashed before my eyes. And somehow, my only thought was that I should have eaten more apple pie."

"Stick on his tail," said Teeny. "He's speeding up!"

I sped up and kept close behind the Corvette as it ducked and weaved its way through light traffic. Zeke's engine moaned like a demon. Mine growled like the king of the jungle. I tried to pull up next to him, but whenever I got close, he hit the gas and pulled out in front of me.

"No need to get in front," said Miss May. "Hang back. Just be sure to keep him in our sights. Traffic's going to pick up here in a few, and we don't want to lose him. You're going to want to stay in the left lane until we pass midtown, then get in the right lane, because people are going to start piling up in the left, trying to exit for Broadway and Times Square."

I did as I was told, casting a surprised look at Miss May. "That was impressive."

"I drove down here every day for years when I worked for the prosecutor's office." Miss May grinned. "And I often made very good time if I don't say so myself."

I did as Miss May had instructed, hanging behind the Corvette three or four cars, never letting it get too far ahead of me. As she'd predicted, traffic soon slowed, and the red Corvette got boxed in by a pair of SUVS.

"Finally, a little breather," said Teeny. "Pull up so we're even with the guy, then Miss May and I will jump out and question him."

"I'm not jumping out of this car in the middle of the West Side Drive," said Miss May. "And there's no shoulder, anyway. This is a two-lane road. Keep it slow and steady for now, Chelsea. He's not going to be able to lose us in stop and go traffic like this."

"Why do you think he's running from us in the first place?" I asked.

"He's running because he's got something to hide," said Miss May, "or he's running because we started chasing him. It's kind of a natural reaction, don't you think?"

"I always run when I think I'm being chased," said Teeny. "I run. I blow my emergency whistle. And I scream 'I've got a gun!' at the top of my lungs."

The red Corvette got over to the left lane. I did the same. "Has that happened a lot?"

"Twice," said Teeny. "Turned out I wasn't being followed either time, but it's better safe than sorry in this big, bad world."

"See, I don't look at the world like that," said Miss May.

"I think the world is fundamentally good. And I think people are fundamentally good, too."

"If that's true, why do people litter?" asked Teeny. "And why do people sell drugs? How come a billion people have gotten murdered in our tiny little town?"

"For a lot of people, the goodness deep down is covered up by a bunch of junk, I think," I said. "Like how the clouds cover the sun in the sky. You know the sun is there, but some days you can't see it."

"Some places go for months without seeing the sun," said Miss May. "I think that's a great way to think about it."

"You two are nuts," said Teeny. "Almost everyone is a no-good, lousy, puddle of scum. That's why when you find your people, you need to stick with them, stay loyal to them, and protect them at all costs."

"This is a weird conversation to have in the middle of a chase," I said.

"Looks like he's getting off at 14th street," said Miss May, gesturing up toward the Corvette with her chin.

"On it." I followed the Corvette into the turn lane and waited for the light to switch to green. "Does this mean we're about to engage in a car chase in the middle of down-town Manhatt—"

Vroom! The Corvette jumped the median before the light turned, darted across traffic and disappeared into the labyrinthine city streets.

"No!" I tried to follow him, but the light changed, and there was no way for me to cross over into the numbered streets without getting side-swiped. I slammed my hand on my horn in frustration. "He got away!"

27

___

GUNNING FOR IT

$\mathcal{I}$ want to tell you that I revved my engine, hopped a curb, located the red Corvette a block away, and got Zeke to confess to murdering Mike. Instead, we cruised around for a while looking for Zeke, then gave up and got pizza.

Ah, yes. The grand old tradition of grabbing pizza any time we were in New York City stood strong that day. Most times we went to the city, we'd go to *John's on Bleecker*. But John's was packed, with a long line out the door, so we went to the nearby *Bleecker Street Pizza* instead.

The place is a classic NY slice joint. The front room is packed with cheap tables and chairs. There are a few cold cases loaded up with cream soda, root beer and water. And five or six guys worked hard behind the counter, tossing dough, pulling pies from the oven, and taking orders.

The three of us grabbed a spot in line behind an NYPD cop who must have been in for an early lunch break. The officer, a muscly Latino guy with close-cropped hair, made small talk with a couple of tourists as he waited for his turn to order.

"Nah, you'll be safe around here," he said. "People come from other parts of the world, they think if you take a stroll in Manhattan you'll get killed. But it's not like that. Actually, New York is one of the safest cities in the country. It's just, when something big happens here, it gets covered globally. Skews the perception of what life is like here."

The tourists, British girls wearing business pants with sensible tops, nodded. "That makes perfect sense," said the taller of the two. "We've been having quite a nice time. Except there were two obnoxious drivers on the West Side Highway on the way here. A red car and a black one having some kind of race."

Teeny gasped and covered her mouth, eyes wide. The cop turned to her. "You OK?"

"Oh yeah," said Teeny. "Just, uh, I saw those drivers too. They were jerks. Both cars were driven by bald men. They were probably angry because they lost their hair. It was like the *Bald and the Furious.*"

The cops and the British women both looked at Teeny as though she were crazy, then, after a few strange seconds, turned back to one another to continue their conversation. I personally refrained from pointing out that Vin Diesel is, in fact, bald, so the moniker could've applied to the actual *Fast and Furious* movies as well. Probably for the best, right?

We placed our order a few minutes later (medium pie, half onions and peppers, half plain), then grabbed a table by the window to sit and wait.

"That girl was talking about us," Teeny whispered. "We were the jerk drivers on the highway. I feel famous."

A server walked by with a fresh-baked pizza. Bubbling cheese. Deep red sauce. Crispy, New York style crust. The smell had that salty, wood-fired, earthiness to it. I stood to get a better look. Teeny tugged at my sleeve.

"Hello?" she said. "Don't you feel famous?"

"I feel eager for pizza," I said. "And I'm also a little annoyed that we lost track of Zeke."

"You think he's a suspect in Mike's murder like, for real?" said Teeny.

"That's why we followed him down here," said Miss May. "The guy clearly has rage issues, and he's furiously hunting for Priscilla. There are so many reasons he might have killed Mike."

"Like what?" said Teeny.

"Maybe Mike was trying to bail on the wedding," I said. "Like he did with me."

Miss May nodded. "Exactly. Zeke doesn't seem like the kind of guy who lets someone hurt his sister and get away with it."

"Maybe he thought Priscilla would be happy about what he did, but then she found out and got so scared of him she went into hiding," I said. "Now Zeke is on the run from the law with no one to turn to, and he's panicking, and he can't find his sister, and..." I trailed off as a red Corvette slowly cruised past the pizza shop. "Wait a second. Is that..."

Miss May stood beside me. "I think it's him!"

Without thinking, I walked outside to get a better look at the Corvette. Sure enough, Zeke was behind the wheel. He was stuck in place for a moment, waiting for a truck to unload in front of him. Then the truck continued on, and so did he. I spotted a rack of Citi Bikes nearby, swiped my credit card and climbed onto the nearest one.

"Chelsea. What are you doing?" said Miss May.

"I'm taking advantage of New York's incredible public biking system to track down Zeke," I said. "Save me a slice."

Zeke's car made a hard right two blocks up ahead. I started pedaling and took off after him. It's incredible, traveling by bike in Manhattan is twice as fast as traveling by car. I'd caught up with the Corvette in ten seconds flat. He had no idea I was following him that time, and I intended to keep it that way. Joining a throng of fellow bikers in the green-painted bike lane, I hung back and did my best to remain inconspicuous.

The red Corvette zipped through a yellow light up ahead. I jammed on my brakes as the light turned red. My fellow cyclists, however, cruised through the red, cautiously looking to make sure no cars were coming in the process.

"I guess we don't stop for reds," I said to myself.

A delivery bike zipped past me, bursting through the red light like a runner exploding through the finish line at a marathon. I followed suit, at a much slower speed, and once again had the Corvette in my eye line.

Slowly but surely, I biked my way through downtown Manhattan. I had one eye on the Corvette and the other on the changing city scape around me. First, we traversed the affluent streets of Greenwich Village, cruising past gorgeous brownstones and beautiful people pushing fancy kids in fancy strollers. Then we were surrounded by NYU students near Washington Square Park, a familiar site after our visit to Professor Green earlier in the investigation. Soon after, we were in New York's grittier Lower East Side, where graffiti was the artistic expression of choice, and men lined the streets drinking from brown bags. The graffiti then gave way to Chinese signage and the smells of fried rice and fish on the wind. We'd arrived in Chinatown and my appetite for pizza suddenly gave way to a desire for plump vegetable dumplings and scallion pancakes.

The red Corvette parked halfway down a Chinatown alleyway. He knocked on a nondescript black door. A neon sign hung above the door. The sign wasn't turned on. but I could read that it said BAR in big, block letters.

The black door opened. Zeke shared a few words with someone I couldn't see. He disappeared inside and the door closed behind him.

Seconds later, the door opened again, and a large man stepped outside. He was built like a Sumo wrestler, and he had a large tattoo crawling from his chest onto his neck.

"Can I help you?" His voice was gruff and thick with suspicion.

I swallowed hard, trying to clear the anxiety from my throat. "Um. I was looking for a bar, but I guess that one is closed." The guy just stood there, looking at me. I had a sense I had stumbled onto something criminal. But I needed to find out for sure. "Can you possibly tell me the time?"

I watched the guy's belt as he lifted his wrist to check his watch. His sports coat lifted a bit to reveal a shiny handgun holstered at his waist.

I muttered "thanks" and hurried away, praying I hadn't drawn more attention to myself than I could afford. The man's eyes drilled a hole in my back as I pedaled away, thinking not of pizza, or dumplings, but instead of that police officer from the pizza shop.

So much for New York being safe.

28

TWO SLICES OF MURDER

"You saved me two slices!?" I sat at the table alongside Teeny and Miss May. A pair of pizza slices stared up at me from a silver tray. I swear, the slices were smiling at me, welcoming me back from my harrowing mission.

"I don't understand. Did you want more than two or are you happy with that number?" said Teeny. "It was a medium pie, so there were only six slices to start. And, as you can see, they're kind of miniature."

"No, no," I said. "Two is plenty."

Teeny shot a look at Miss May. "Told you we only needed to save the one."

"Can we maybe talk about the angry brother you just chased down?" said Miss May. "I love pizza as much as the next girl, but seriously."

That first bite of pizza was perfect. The homemade mozzarella was lightly salted and perfectly creamy. The San Marzano tomato sauce added an incredible tang. The crust was somehow chewy and crunchy at the same time. "I'd rather talk about the pizza," I said.

Miss May glared at me. I washed down my pizza with a big glug of cream soda and jumped into the story of my bicycle chase through Manhattan. Miss May and Teeny stopped to compare notes at every neighborhood I mentioned, seemingly in competition for the "who knows New York best" award. When I got to the part about the gun, Teeny stood and paced, running her hands through her platinum blonde locks.

"What happened next?" she said.

I shrugged. "Nothing really. I came here. Ate pizza."

"No one followed you?" said Teeny.

The thought hadn't occurred to me. For a second, I doubted my sleuthing abilities. Why hadn't I cast a single glance over my shoulder? Why hadn't it occurred to me to employ some evasive maneuvers just in case Zeke had given pursuit? Was I a sleuth or just some small-town baker in over her head?

"If they'd chased her, they would have caught up to her by now," said Miss May. "No offense, Chelsea. You're not exactly lady Lance Armstrong on the Citi Bike."

"How about we take a break from insulting me and talk about what this all might mean," I said. "Seems to me Zeke is some kind of criminal. And if he was that desperate to locate Priscilla, there's a decent likelihood she was caught up in the crimes right alongside him."

Miss May grabbed a discarded crust from the tray and took a bite, chewing thoughtfully. "You think they're a crime family, then."

"I'm not saying they're mafia or something." I wiped my mouth with a napkin, grabbing for my second slice. "But we can assume they were close, right? Otherwise, Zeke wouldn't have been so freaked out that he couldn't find her for a couple of days."

"Good point," said Teeny. "My sister Peach could be missing right now. I don't know. We haven't linked up in forever. But if we were tight like we used to be, and she went missing, I'd have known in less than a day." She frowned. "Oh no. Are Peach and I growing apart?"

"Relationships ebb and flow," said Miss May, tossing the words out dismissively. "Zeke and Priscilla are the siblings we need to focus on right now. Chelsea, what do you think we do next?"

"Get more pizza?" I gave Miss May a forced smile. She did not smile back. "You're not in the mood, I get it. Let me think. Man, this all feels so much more dangerous now. And it feels way more important that we find Priscilla and talk to her about all this. It's possible Zeke is after her for some reason. In which case, she'd have to be hiding someplace he'd never look for her." I sat up straight as a realization hit me. "Or she'd have to be hiding someplace he fears."

Teeny gasped. "Right!" She leaned forward. "Wait. What?"

"I have an idea where Priscilla might be." I snatched the crust from Miss May and chomped down on it like a cigar. "Let's go, girls. It's party time."

I charged out of the pizza place. Miss May and Teeny followed behind me, muttering about my 'party time' line. Rolling my eyes, I called back, "It's my new catchphrase! Get used to it!"

"But it's not good," said Miss May. "Actually, it's kind of a cliché."

"Sorry, Auntie," I said, winking at Miss May for perhaps the first time ever. "Whether you like it or not: it's party time!"

I set off down the street, feeling sassy and strong. Then

came the black ice. And the bruised elbow. And the reminder that winking is not for me.

29

BEEF GHERKY

*W*e got to the Gherkin residence mid-afternoon. The house was a gorgeous old colonial perched atop the Blue Mountain Cliffs. This is the type of place the children of doctors and lawyers grow up, looking out over the little people, saying, "If those little people worked like I have, they'd be up here, too."

The drive up to the home took us up a winding road that at times felt like a vertical climb. Though I was aware of the magnificent vista to my left, I didn't dare look out over it for fear of losing sight of the road and causing me, Teeny, and Miss May to plummet to a loud and uncomfortable death.

Besides, the two of them described the view in such awed detail that I didn't feel I needed to turn my head to get a good understanding of what was over there.

"Oh, my goodness! The river looks so dark blue from up here!"

"You can see the big, gray clouds reflected in the water."

"The mountains are ugly with no leaves on the trees, like creepy little bald monks."

I parked at the foot of the Gherkin driveway, beside a

handcrafted mailbox that had been built into a stone wall, like some kind of mail kiln. As I looked up at the home, a series of memories stung my mind in such quick succession it was like I'd stepped on a hornet's nest. I saw the first time Mike brought me home to meet his parents. He'd told me to hide my sense of humor, and he'd warned me not to eat dessert, cuz then they'd think I was gross. I was like, "Why are they going to offer me dessert if they think dessert is for gross people?" He'd ignored the question in order to pull a brush out of his pocket and flatten my frizzy hair. Next, I saw the Christmas Mike and I were supposed to have the house to ourselves. It had started out nice, then he'd invited all his high school friends over to play drinking games. They accidentally locked me in the basement and couldn't hear my calls for help over their music, so I had gotten stuck down there for almost six hours with nothing to do.

The memories kept coming as we walked up the driveway toward the home. The place looked cozy from a distance, with a Christmas tree glowing in a front room and a peaceful candle in every window, but I knew better than that. Every member of Mike's family was prideful, difficult, and chaotic. Sometimes those traits were hidden, but I'd seen them all at their worst.

Why had I decided to visit these people, again? Oh, right. My hunch told me Priscilla was boarded up inside. Zeke never would have thought to look for Priscilla with her not-quite in-laws. And Priscilla and the Gherkins shared a certain aloof snobbishness. I had a hunch they might get along.

Mrs. Abigail Gherkin opened the front door before we made it all the way up the front path. She wore a red and green holiday dress and a string of pearls that were only half a shade whiter than her perfect teeth.

"Chelsea. Um, hello." She gave me a tight smile. "Teeny. Miss May."

"Hi." I returned her smile with a genuine one, hoping to soften the matriarch as much as possible. She'd never liked me, and I knew I'd have to earn her trust if she was going to lead me to Priscilla. "We're just here to pay our respects. It's so terrible what happened to Mike."

Mike's dad, Edward, came and stood at Abigail's side. He lowered his bifocals to the tip of his nose when he saw me. The two of them looked like they'd just stepped away from dinner with John F. Kennedy in 1960, all wide-eyed innocence and perfectly pressed Christmas formalwear.

I know. It's not cool to hate on people who just lost their son. Nor is it cool to hate on people generally. But they think dessert is for 'gross people.' Try to keep that in mind.

Edward scoffed and sipped his martini with disdain. "Pay your respects. Right. We know about the note that was left at the scene of the crime."

"Chelsea did not kill your son," said Miss May, stepping forward. "If she was going to do that, she would have done it years ago, after he humiliated her in front of all her family and friends."

I looked down. It had been a while, but to hear it put so baldly sent a pang of shame harpooning through my body.

"Yeah!" said Teeny, eyes big and angry. "Also, Chelsea has investigated more than a dozen murders. If she was going to kill him, she wouldn't have left a note incriminating herself. And the whole scene would have been a lot less messy."

Edward set down his martini. "I'll show you messy!"

"Hold on, hold on," I held up the whites of my palms in place of a white flag of surrender. "This is all getting way out of control. We're here to offer condolences, and—"

"Yeah, right," said Abigail.

I pushed forward. "We're also here because we're investigating Mike's murder. We want to find out who did this so they can be punished. Mike deserves that. We all do."

Mike's parents stared at me so hard I thought their heads might explode. But I was too caught up in what I'd just said for their looks to bother me. It had just hit me that I wanted to find justice for Mike more than I did for most victims. I made eye contact with Abigail. "I loved him."

She looked down. "We all did."

"What are you doing here?" A rageful voice spoke from somewhere behind Mike's parents. They parted to make way for a twenty-something man I only vaguely recognized as Mike's cousin, Ryker.

"She's investigating Michael's murder," said Abigail.

As the young man got closer, I noticed a flat, emotionless look in his vacant brown eyes. His eyebrows were only a few millimeters from a unibrow, and he wore a t-shirt with a wolf on it. "Did I hear you say you loved my cousin?" he said.

"Ryker—" said Edward.

Ryker cut him off. "If she loved him, she would have gone after him."

"What are you talking about, kid? Mike left her at the altar." Teeny hooked her arm in mine. I could feel her shaking with anger. I put my hand on hers to try to calm her.

"People don't do that kind of thing unless they're going through something very hard emotionally," said Ryker. "Mike was struggling, and you just let him leave you there."

Abigail turned back to Ryker. "That's enough, Ryker."

Ryker clammed up as soon as Abigail reprimanded him.

I took a step forward. "Look. We're just here looking for

Priscilla, OK? We think she could be in danger, and it could be connected to this case. I have reason to believe she's staying with you. If that's true, could you just let her know we're here?"

"Priscilla isn't staying here," said Edward. "We haven't seen her since before...what happened."

"That's interesting." Miss May nodded toward the foyer. "Those are her shoes there in your foyer."

30

SHOE'S OFF

*A*bigail and Edward protested. Ryker, weirdo that he was, tried to pass it off like the pair of pink-accented sneakers were his. Teeny, Miss May and I just stood there, taking it all in, as they tripped over themselves. At one point, Edward said "Ryker loves his dainty little tennis shoes. Isn't that right, Ryker? You have quite the progressive taste when it comes to tennis shoes!"

Ryker agreed and crossed over to the shoes, trying to shove his feet into the minuscule toe boxes. I suppose that was the point at which it all got to be too much for her, because just as Ryker jammed the entirety of his right foot into the shoe, Priscilla appeared at the top of the steps. She dabbed at the corners of her eyes. I wondered if she'd been crying.

"Enough of this craziness," she said. "You're all very sweet for trying to shield me from this. But they're clearly not buying this shoe charade. I think the best way to get them to leave me alone is if I just talk to them."

"You're grieving, sweetheart," said Abigail. "That's not fair to you."

Sweetheart!? Really!? Abigail Gherkin had barely looked me in the eye during my time dating Mike. What was so bad about me, anyway? Was I too short for him? Not exotic enough? Did I not fit in with their stupid, snobby, elitist—

Priscilla's graceful walk down the spiral staircase broke me out of my raged-out fantasy land. The woman was like a flamingo. She somehow looked elegant and alien at the same time, which is, I suppose, the quality she had that I lacked. I'm nothing if not completely and unquestionably human, in all my doughy glory.

"We're all grieving," said Priscilla. The way she spoke I suddenly felt like I was in a play from the 1940s. Her chin, pointed up just a fraction of an inch, gave Priscilla the haughty air of an old-timey movie star. Flapping gently behind her, a satin nightgown hugged her figure in all the right places and strengthened Priscilla's old Hollywood vibes. "Chelsea, Teeny, and Miss May wouldn't be here if it wasn't important. Maybe there's something I know that can help them catch this killer once and for all."

Miss May was right, I thought. *This girl does not seem like a chef at all.* Nowhere to be seen was the gruff forthrightness I'd found in every other chef I'd ever met. I couldn't imagine her covered in flower or egg or chocolate sauce, either. But I suppose that was the annoying thing about women like Priscilla. They lived lives just like the rest of us. The only difference was that they somehow managed to avoid the mess.

Dead boyfriends are messy. I know. And I tried to keep compassion in mind as Priscilla floated toward us. But she was just so... Stinking... Perfect.

The four of us gathered in what Abigail Gherkin referred to as 'the drawing room,' which was a den, adjacent to the foyer, that had been decorated with antique French furniture, mirrors and ornate ceramics.

"You just let us know if you need anything, sweetheart." Abigail gave Priscilla a kind smile as she exited, closing the door behind her.

Just like that, Teeny, Miss May and I were face-to-face with Priscilla. Us, with our normal bone structure and standard chins. Priscilla with her... Big Priscilla energy.

"What would you like to ask me?" she said, raising her eyebrows expectantly.

The authoritative tone she took surprised me. I looked over at Miss May, who stammered and pulled at her collar. "Well, I guess, we were just hoping..."

"We wanted to ask you about people you knew," said Teeny, looking equally off guard.

"I know so many people," said Priscilla, adjusting the position of a coaster on the coffee table. "Be more specific."

"I'd like to know if you have any siblings," I said. "A brother, maybe?"

"Don't tell me you met Zeke." Priscilla sighed. My question had chipped her armor. Suddenly she seemed much more human... Much more wounded.

"We were looking for you at your restaurant," said Teeny. "Cute place, by the way. How do find so many tattooed people to work as servers?"

"In my experience once you get close enough to New York City you can have your pick of tattooed staff," said Priscilla. "I find they bring an edgy vibe to the place that makes it more attractive to day-tripping city people, though I'd never get a tattoo myself. What did Zeke do now?"

Her voice quavered a bit as she said her brother's name. I wondered why. And the way she emphasized the word 'now' was curious, too.

"Has Zeke gotten into a lot of trouble in his life?" I asked.

"He's—" She looked away. "He's my only family. But he's mentally ill. Bipolar. Borderline something disorder. He's got it all."

Miss May nodded. "That must have been hard, growing up with someone like that."

"Harder for him than it was for me." Priscilla picked at the edge of the coaster she'd only moments before set straight on the table. "He's gotten into plenty of trouble, yes. Not sure he's ever not been in trouble, in one way or another. I have fifty missed calls from him. Voicemails. He's convinced I'm going to be killed next. I told him you have more to be afraid of than I do, Chelsea. The killer framed you. They didn't want anything to do with me."

"You believe I'm innocent?" I said.

Priscilla looked down. "No reason for you to have killed Mike. Not now. Not after all these years." She made eye contact with me. "I was upset that night that you found him."

"I understand," I said.

Priscilla's energy shifted suddenly as she flattened both her palms on her thighs. "OK, then. Enough small talk. What else do you need to know?"

Miss May explained that we wanted to know more about Mike's life. Had he gotten into any recent arguments at work? Had he made any enemies it might help for us to know about? The more questions she asked, the further Priscilla's face sank.

"He made enemies everywhere he went," she said. "My therapist told me it was because he had what's called an 'authoritarian personality.' People either fall in line, or they fight back. There's not much in between. I fell in line."

"Me, too." I felt more connected to Priscilla in that

moment than I had to anyone in such a long time. "But I thought you two were happy. Why were you in therapy?"

"Everything. Life." She gestured out toward the main house with her eyes. "This family."

I scooted to the edge of my chair. "Abigail called you sweetheart. She loves you."

Priscilla laughed to herself. "She loves me as long as I present myself like a 'Gherkin', whatever that means. But if I make any of my true opinions known? If I refuse to sign her stupid pre-nup. If I dare go to a family function wearing something she doesn't like... Edward doesn't have the spine to stand up to her. Mike didn't, either." There was a long pause as Priscilla shook her head. Her chin quivered and the sides of her mouth turned down. "After kick boxing that night, I sat in the parking lot of the dojo and I called my therapist. Kick boxing was supposed to help me feel better. But I still felt anxious after. Sat out there and talked to my stupid shrink for half an hour. If I'd gone straight home... If I'd been there... Mike wouldn't have... The killer... They wouldn't have..."

Miss May put a hand on Priscilla's knee as Priscilla broke down in tears. "You'd both be dead, sweetie. There's nothing you could have done."

Priscilla broke down into a heavy sob. Miss May and Teeny jumped in to comfort her. I was stuck in the past about thirty seconds, thinking about what Priscilla had said about the Gherkins, and Mike's horrible mother.

If anyone in the world was evil enough to kill their own family member, it was a Gherkin. And I was sitting in their drawing room.

31

POWDER ROOM KEG

I know. There are plenty of ladylike ways to excuse yourself to go to the bathroom.

"May I use your powder room?"

"Pardon me. Could you point me in the direction of the ladies' room?"

"Sorry to interrupt, but could I possibly make use of your lavatory?" |

But no matter which eloquent, old-timey phrase I used, when I asked to use the bathroom, it always sounded like I was about to have an emergency. That night at the Gherkin house, the emergency was that I wanted to sneak out of the drawing room to snoop around the home, unnoticed.

"I'm sorry, I gotta go to the bathroom. I mean... May I? The powder room, if you don't mind. Kindly please and thank you." I stood abruptly.

Priscilla narrowed her eyes while slowly pointing out toward the hall. "Down the hall. First door on your left."

I made eye contact with Miss May as I exited. My eyes said "That was weird. Don't worry. I'm fully aware."

Her eyes said, "Wow. You're totally right. That was a bizarre way to go to the bathroom."

Then I made things worse. "I don't need to know where it is," I said. "I've been here a bunch of times before. I've used this bathroom more times than I've been to Washington D.C. And I've been to Washington D.C. four times." *I'd forgotten that I already knew where the bathroom was and was doing my best to cover it up. Weird, weird, weird.*

I tripped over my own feet as I exited, as if, somehow, I needed one more exclamation mark on the sentence that was my odd behavior. Then, thankfully, I was alone in the Gherkin's grand entryway.

The bathroom beckoned to me from down the hall. Though I'd fabricated the need to go so I'd have an excuse to leave, I suddenly really had to pee. The little powder room was just as I remembered it. One entire wall was a floral painting with a heavy, bronze frame. And the toilet opened and closed on its own while whispering something in Japanese.

I'm not even kidding. The toilet spoke Japanese.

I did my business nice and quick, muttered a deferential "Arigato" to the bowl, and hurried back into the hall. Bam. I ran right into cousin Ryker.

"What are you doing?" he said.

I'd always thought Ryker was much younger than me and Mike. Maybe that's because he'd only just graduated from college when I'd met him. But I wasn't too far from college at that time, either, and there in the hall I noticed signs of aging I'd never spotted before.

Ryker was gray at the temples, with more flecks of gray in his beard. He had subtle crow's feet around the sides of his eyes, and his jawline had softened considerably to make way for what Teeny always called 'the dreaded turkey neck.'

Suddenly I questioned whether he was younger than me at all. I don't like to be judgmental, but the following is merely an observation: the guy did not look good.

"I was just in the bathroom," I said, gesturing back toward the elegant Japanese toilet with which I'd just finished chatting. "Figured it was only polite to say hi to the toilet since I was here. She and I always got along well back in the day."

It was a joke. Ryker either didn't get it or he hated jokes. Or he hated me. All three seemed like distinct possibilities.

A floorboard creaked upstairs. The yellow light from the chandelier cast triangular reflections on the wall behind Ryker. I braced myself for a hostile conversation.

"I live here now," Ryker said. "I work at the video game store at the big mall down county."

"Nice. Wow, awesome," I said. "Do you get to play games at work?"

"I don't know. Did you kill my cousin?"

Wow. That was the non-sequitur to end all non-sequiturs, I thought. *Fair, though, considering the note. And our history. And Ryker's healthy sense of angry suspicion.*

"I did not," I said.

"You didn't go after him when he left you at the altar."

"I did not. And I know you think that wasn't kind of me. But think about it from my perspective. I mean, I'd just been left at the altar. You were there. Can you imagine how embarrassing that was for me?"

"You got very red when you realized he wasn't coming."

"I bet," I said.

"You got even more red when the priest asked you to call him up. Then I saw you at the hotel the next morning and you looked like you'd been crying."

"I had been crying," I said.

"But people don't leave their wives standing there unless said people are hurting on the inside."

I got choked up, out of nowhere. Ryker, in all of his bluntness, had stumbled across an idea I'd never considered: Mike had been hurting. People don't hurt other people unless they hurt themselves. I'd never thought of Mike with such humanity before.

Regret, shame, and disappointment swirled in my chest. "I guess you're right. Honestly, I never thought of it that way. Never checked on Mike. Never thought I had a reason to."

"He wasn't a happy guy. One time, last year, he yelled at me because I fell asleep at family dinner. Family dinners are boring. Remember? One time you came to one and you brought a casserole, but Aunt Abigail was allergic, and it was a big problem."

"I was hoping you'd all forgotten about that."

"Oh no, not at all," said Ryker. "Any time anyone mentions tree nuts, Aunt Abigail says 'I almost died that Christmas. I know I'd told Chelsea about my allergies. I think she wanted to kill me!'"

I sighed. "She had told me. But I forgot."

"You have been open and honest in this conversation, so I no longer think you killed my cousin," said Ryker, matter-of-factly. "Now you better get back into the drawing room. If you spend all your snooping time talking to me, pretty soon Priscilla's going to start to wonder where you are."

I nodded. "Good point. Nice talking to you, Ryker."

He walked away without saying anything, placing each foot down with such care it looked like he was trying to avoid cracks in the sidewalk. Ryker was clearly the odd man out in the Gherkin family. All families have one, don't they?

Like Zeke, for instance.

32

CHRISTMAS COWBOY

*W*ayne was out front waiting for us when we got to the *Brown Cow* that night. He had his thumbs hitched in his belt like an old-school cowboy and he gave us a little head nod as we approached.

I quickened my pace, hurried toward him, and gave him a big hug. "Howdy, partner."

For a second, the backdrop of Pine Grove fell into the distance and was replaced by a dusty Texas landscape. Wayne's police car, which was parked nearby, transformed into a gorgeous black horse. And Wayne's voice was suddenly tinged with a Texan accent.

"Howdy," he said. "Hope you ladies stayed safe out there today. Especially you, Miss Chelsea. Beauty as fine as yours needs to be protected, that's what I always say."

I stammered. Suddenly, Imaginary Cowboy Wayne was chewing on a long piece of straw. One blink later and he was unbuttoning the top two buttons on his shirt, with a deep sigh. "Hot out there, ain't it? Hope y'all don't mind if I cool off a bit."

His muscles: rippling.

My eyes: wide.

My hands: on his chest.

The sun: setting in the distance, casting a long shadow over the gorgeous Texas countryside.

Miss May: smacking me in the back of the head. "I asked you what you want to drink, Chelsea. I'm assuming something decaf."

Just like that, we were back in Pine Grove, Wayne was wearing a fully-buttoned shirt, and everyone was looking at me like I was out of my mind. I stammered. "Um... Uh... Yeah. Sure."

Wayne held the door open and stepped aside for me to enter. "After you."

I gave him a weak smile. Wayne was a modern-day gentleman, most of the time. But boy, oh boy, did I want that cowboy back, just for a second.

We settled in with our coffees at a table in the far corner of the café. It was near closing time, so the three of us were the only customers in the shop. Brian tidied up behind the coffee bar, humming Christmas tunes to himself. The air smelled like the peppermint mochas he'd surely been making all day. And the marshmallow in my hot cocoa bobbed like a plump little iceberg, waiting to be eaten.

"Priscilla is staying with the Gherkins," I said to Wayne. "She thinks if she would have gotten home sooner, she could have prevented Mike's death."

"Statistically, she likely would have been murdered, too," said Wayne.

"That's what we said," said Teeny. "I've seen it time and time again. Someone stumbles into the carriage house while a murder is taking place, then they get murdered too. No killer is trying to make their murders a public affair, especially not with the nosy Garden Club poking their head around every Thursday, digging things up near the back house."

"I know that's *Jenna and Mr. Flowers* because only your British shows have carriage houses and garden clubs," I said.

"Wow, Chelsea, you really are a sleuth," said Teeny. "That's spot on!"

"How about you apply those skills to the actual murder of your actual ex in your actual small-town?" said Miss May. "I'm not trying to ruin the fun here, but that visit to the Gherkin house was unsettling."

"Why?" Wayne leaned forward, sipping his drink.

"Because they're all so unsettled," said Miss May. "Priscilla is beside herself. The mom is worse than Cinderella's stepmother. So snobby and uptight. The dad is just the same. And the cousin—"

"The cousin has more of a heart than I realized at first," I said.

"He and Chelsea bonded in the Japanese bathroom," Teeny explained to Wayne.

"Everybody slow down a beat," said Wayne. "Take me through the entire visit, minute by minute."

He listened as we spoke, then asked if Priscilla had explained why she hadn't attended Mike's services.

Me, Teeny and Miss May shrugged in unison.

"Totally forgot to ask about that," Teeny said. "Whoops?"

"I was assuming she was too sad to get out of bed," I said. "Depression is a real thing, you know. It can hit you at any time. One minute you're taking a bite of a panini, the next minute you're lying in bed and you don't know why, but you don't want to do any of your chores."

"What happens to the panini?" said Miss May.

"Not important," I said, keeping my focus on Wayne.

"We didn't ask, but it seemed obvious. She was feeling upset and guilty for not getting back to the Mike sooner on the day that he died."

"She was having an emergency therapy session," said Teeny. "That's why she wasn't home."

"And why is she living with the Gherkins now?" said Wayne. "This crazy brother is her only family?"

"I don't think you're supposed to say 'crazy' to refer to the mentally ill," said Teeny. "I saw a segment about it on *The Today Show*."

"The Gherkins are pretty much all she has," I said, confirming Wayne's theory. "As far as we know, they're her only family other than the one brother. And they're not even technically in the same family. But they were far nicer to her than they ever were to me."

"Did that upset you?" said Wayne, sitting up a little straighter.

"No. I just don't know why they didn't like me."

"Because you're a human woman, not a robot like one of them," said Miss May.

"The way you three are talking about Mike's parents... I don't know..." Wayne trailed off.

I shook my head. "I thought about this. They are unpleasant people. But I don't think they did it.There's no way he was killed by his own parents. Mike was the golden child of the entire extended family. They were obsessed with him, obsessed with his accomplishments. His parents would have sooner killed themselves than hurt their only son."

"And did Priscilla point you toward any new suspects?" said Wayne. "That's why you went there, right?"

"I was talking to Ryker most of the time," I said.

Miss May took a big sip of her coffee and set it down

gently. "We asked Priscilla if Mike had any additional enemies while Chelsea was out of the room. She said Mike kept his life completely sealed off from her. Sometimes she heard him yelling on his work phone, but he'd never tell her why or with whom he was speaking. Same deal for almost every detail of his life. He kept everything important to him under lock and key."

That phrase 'lock and key' rang in my ears. Mike hadn't been quite as private with me, but he had always been careful not to mix our lives too much. I'd met Frank and Steven, for instance, but had never been introduced to his other friends. And there was an air of secrecy about Mike that I'd never quite put my finger on until Miss May had uttered that phrase... I had been about to marry someone I'd known so little about.

How had I gotten to that place? And why had I said yes when he'd proposed to me?

33

LOCK AND KEY

"*A*ll dreams are memories from a life forgotten."
I'm not sure where I heard that quote, but ever since I'd dreamt about Mike and his safe, it had stuck with me. I knew I'd always felt odd about Mike's secret safe. But I couldn't remember... Had the two of us argued about its contents in real life, or only in my nightmares? Had I really begged for him to let me see inside?

Now that Mike was gone, the safe felt like a symbol for so many of the problems between us. There was information he had, that he never felt the need to share with me. That kind of communication can't work in a relationship, and it certainly can't work in a marriage.

Had he known he wasn't going to make it to the altar on our wedding day? Or he been so out of touch with his emotions that he was taken by surprise just as I was? Or was he such a bad communicator that the only way he could figure out how to break up with me was to leave me standing there like a fool in front of all my family and friends?

These are the thoughts that ran through my head when

it hit the pillow that night. I think, if I had a therapist, he'd have warned me that ruminating on the unchangeable past never leads to happiness. But what would that therapist have said of dreams and their power to point to the truth?

As I finally drifted off that evening, I was whisked back to the apartment Mike and I had shared in the city. This time we stood in the kitchen. I wore my favorite apron, pink, polka-dotted with chocolate cupcakes. Mike wore business casual clothes.

In the dream he'd not yet set his sights on my interior design business and had instead been out interviewing for jobs at tech companies all day.

"These guys look at me like I'm some kind of loser," he said. "They ask one question, and then another, and another. I know they're not going to hire me. Why are they wasting my time?"

"How do you know they're not going to hire you?" I checked on a loaf of bread in the oven. It was dream bread, so it was a big, crusty loaf that looked like a page from *Beautiful Bread Monthly*.

"Because they haven't hired me yet!"

"...how would they have hired you before they interviewed you? And why would they be interviewing you if they knew they didn't want to hire you?"

"These guys just go on power trips up and down the east coast. They go from one great school to the next, interviewing the top graduates, even though they only pick the very best student from each university. Then they do the same thing in big cities. They go through the pile of resumes, decide who they're going to hire, then call everyone in anyways, just so they can feel powerful."

"Wow. You really don't trust these people."

"Why would I? They work at the biggest banks in America."

"You want to work for them," I said. "But you don't trust them?"

Mike charged into the next room. The orange glow from my previous dream was back, as were the 97 yowling cats. Mike kicked off his shoes, sending them flying into the corner. A dozen cats scattered.

"I told you I don't want to take care of these animals. They're disgusting. And why won't they shut up?"

The *Goldfinger* poster caught my eye. It vibrated with some kind of cosmic energy, so much so that I could almost see sound waves passing through it. I walked toward it, compelled by some kind of outside force. Calmness overtook my body, despite Mike's anger.

"I need to see inside this safe."

"Chelsea—"

"Now, Mike." I walked toward the poster. It was huge but it felt weightless in my hands as I removed it from the wall. I handed it to Mike. The twilight of my calm had stupefied him. He watched in silence as I began to spin the dial on the safe.

Click. Click. Click. Click. Click.

"Chelsea..." He spoke almost inaudibly. "That's my... My... You can't..."

"Shh!"

"No." He threw his body between me and the safe. His eyes were glazed over. He looked drugged. But then the energy suddenly rushed through his body and he stood straight up. "No, no, no!"

He let out a primal scream. I stood there, unblinking and unafraid.

"You can't have my art!" he said.

"So it's art, then," I said.

"No. What?"

"You have art in the safe." He didn't respond. I repeated myself over and over, looking him straight in the eye. "You have art in the safe. You have art in the safe. You have art in the safe. You have art—"

Bam! I woke up, sweaty and gasping for breath. "Art... Safe..." Steve the dog scooted toward me and licked my face. Moonlight streamed in through my window. I felt as though I'd had a massive breakthrough, and I hoped Teeny and Miss May would help me figure out what it all meant.

34

PANCAKES AND PANDEMONIUM

I'd woken up in the middle of the frozen night. I wanted nothing more than to tell Miss May all about my dream as soon as possible. Without thinking, I hurried to her bedroom. The sound of the ticking grandfather clock downstairs stopped me just before I walked inside, and suddenly my mind was reprimanding me for considering waking up my elderly aunt just to tell her about my scary dream.

"You're a grown woman," said the mind. "Go back to bed. You can tell Miss May all about it in the morning. There's nothing she can do right now anyway."

By the time I got back to bed, little Steve was already snoring, curled up like a snail on top of my favorite pillow. The weight of the dream was still heavy on my shoulders at that point, but I managed a laugh at the sight of the dog.

"If you weren't so cute, I'd never let you steal my spot," I said, sliding into the bed beside him.

I drifted off to sleep listening to the sound of Steve's steady, rhythmic breathing. When I woke, I found a note on the kitchen counter from Miss May.

"Went out! If you can't figure out where I am, you're not such a good sleuth after all. Love, YWA (Your Wonderful Aunt)"

Cold coffee in the pot. Old bread in the breadbasket. Wedding anxiety swirling with mystery anxiety in the pit of my stomach. I needed comfort food, and I had a hunch Miss May had had the same idea.

A trio of carolers greeted me outside *Grandma's* with a booming rendition of "Deck the Halls." Tom Gigley led the troupe with his enthusiastic baritone. He was flanked by a couple of guys I recognized from around town, and the three of them sang together in perfect harmony. An elderly couple danced along to the song a few feet away, moving in unison like they must have on their wedding day, but it was too cold for me to appreciate the music for long. I tossed a few bucks in the charity bucket and hurried inside with a big smile.

I found Teeny and Miss May at our booth, arguing.

"This is a token of my appreciation." Miss May shoved an envelope across the table towards Teeny. "You have to take it."

"Absolutely not!" Teeny shoved the envelope back toward Miss May. "I don't give you free food all year just so you can pay me for it at the holidays. I give it to you because I love you."

"And I'm giving you this holiday gift because I love you." The envelope scratched along the table as Miss May shoved it back.

"No!" said Teeny. "Your token of appreciation is ruining my token of appreciation!"

"I'll take the money," I said, reaching for the envelope with a smile.

"Very funny, Chelsea." Miss May took the envelope and

tucked it back in her purse, giving Teeny the stink eye. "I'll find a way to get this to you, one way or another."

Ignoring Miss May's threat, Teeny patted the seat beside her and looked up at me. "Plop down, girly. We've got mysteries to solve."

I sat where Teeny had indicated. "Have you two –"

"Ordered pancakes already," said Teeny. "They should be here any minute."

"Before we got distracted, Teeny and I were talking about our run-in with Priscilla at the Gherkin residence," said Miss May.

"What about it?" I asked.

"Why was Priscilla staying with them in the first place?" said Teeny.

"Her only other family is her mentally-ill brother," I said.

"That's what I said," said Miss May, shooting a look at Teeny.

"I get that," said Teeny. "But wouldn't you rather live anywhere than with the Gherkins?"

I stammered. "It's hard to say. "Priscilla just lost Mike. Being there, with his family, probably makes her feel closer to him. And I don't imagine her brother has a nice place. He's some kind of criminal. I don't imagine he's got a Japanese toilet and hand soap from *Bloomingdale's*."

"I agree," said Miss May. "Now will you tell me why you came to my door at three in the morning, stood there, then plodded away without coming in to talk to me?"

My face flushed. "Didn't realize you knew I was there. Why didn't you say anything?"

"I like to let people come to me in their own time."

Miss May's little smirk forced one of my involuntary eye rolls. "That's annoying."

Miss May shrugged. "So what's up?"

I told them all about my dream, concluding with the suspicion that Mike had been storing highly valuable art in the safe. Once I was all done, Teeny wrinkled her nose. "I'm confused. Did you see the art in real life?"

"Well, no." I said.

"Did you see it in the dream?" said Teeny.

"Not really, but—"

"I think Chelsea's on to something," said Miss May. "His house was gauche, but Mike had an eye for beauty. He loved Chelsea. He recognized her skill in interior design. And he comes from a family that's clearly obsessed with the aesthetics of their life, very concerned with having the finer things."

"Hence the Murakami-reciting toilet bowl," I said.

Miss May pointed right at me. It felt good. "Exactly."

"Are you getting to a plan here or what?" said Teeny. "Sorry. That was aggressive. I want my pancakes."

"Old Mrs. Vanderhoot is the biggest art collector in the county," said Miss May. "I saw a special on PBS about her last year. Some think she has the most extensive collection of fine art in the state."

"Do you know her?" said Teeny.

Miss May grinned as Petey set our pancakes down on the table. "She buys her Christmas tree from me every year."

35

GIVE A HOOT

*M*rs. Vanderhoot opened the door halfway and peered out at us with narrowed eyes. Her name and reputation as an art aficionado had led me to expect a woman wearing a flowing Asian nightgown, sipping a morning martini, and speaking with a faux British accent. But the lady Vanderhoot was far more reserved, with cropped, graying hair and thick black glasses.

"I haven't murdered anyone," she said, jaw set tight.

"That's not why we're here, Miranda," said Miss May. "May we come in?"

Miss May moved to enter the home. Miranda Vanderhoot didn't move an inch of her imposing figure. Miss May gave her a polite smile and returned to her rightful place out on the porch.

"Actually," said Teeny, raising a pointer finger in the air, "we're here to talk about—"

"You three don't know Picasso from Popeye," said Miranda. "You can't claim you're here to talk about art."

"That's where you're wrong," said Miss May. "My niece here is a trained interior designer. She took several art history courses in college. I'm sure she could tell the difference."

I gave the strong-featured older woman a small smile. "Picasso is the one who gets strong from gobbling up cans of spinach, right?"

"I like you." Her eyes were trained on me, but her tone was so flat I found it hard to believe.

"Oh, uh, thanks," I said.

"Don't say 'oh' or 'um'," said Miranda. "Those words mean nothing. If you speak them, they render you meaningless. As women, we must fight for every ounce of meaning in this world. To give it away through lazy speech is a travesty." *She wasn't wrong. But we were not there to talk about the challenges facing modern-day women.* "Your husband was just murdered," she continued. "My goodness, my manners. And my condolences."

"Ex," I said. "We never quite made it to husband and wife. I appreciate that, though. Indubitably."

I'd included that last word, 'indubitably,' to make up for my prior stuttering. Miranda Vanderhoot picked up on it without missing a moment. "Adding unnecessarily complicated words to your speech does as much damage as the filler words you used earlier."

I nodded, suddenly eager not only for the woman to like me, but also for her to think I was a good student. With a flash, years of 'teacher's pet' training came back to me, and I found the instincts too strong to fight.

"Yes, Mrs. Vanderhoot," I said. "I understand."

Teeny and Miss May exchanged a confused look, then turned back to Vanderhoot in unison.

"We need to know if any new art has hit the market in the aftermath of Michael Gherkin's murder," said Miss May.

"You have your ear to the proverbial canvas, so we figured we'd ask you."

"You want me to provide inside information on the art market," said the stately older woman. "My access to information is what gives me an edge, you understand?"

"We won't tell anyone your trade secrets," said Teeny.

"Yet I don't remember learning to trust you," said Vanderhoot.

"You've bought your Christmas trees from me every year since you moved to the area," said Miss May. "Have you ever found me to be anything less than reliable, professional and trustworthy?"

"And you're clearly aware of our accomplishments as amateur sleuths," I said. "Plus, you said it yourself, we wouldn't know good art if it bonked us in the head."

Vanderhoot opened the door a few inches further. "Fine. You may come inside."

After quite a bit of back and forth, Mrs. Miranda Vanderhoot admitted that a Rembrandt had hit the market the day after Mike's murder. She said the seller had listed the piece on the dark web, which indicated it might have been procured illegally, or have questionable lineage. Further evidence of the questionable procurement was that the seller was asking far too much for the piece which, though rare, was not from one of Rembrandt's more sought-after eras. According to Vanderhoot, the piece was a portrait of a man looking at the painter with a look of disgust. She said the painting was true to Rembrandt's general interest in ugliness over beauty, and that it was a masterwork in both light and shade.

Just before we left, and after much convincing, Vanderhoot used her personal account to set up an art meetup between me, Teeny, Miss May, and the art dealer the next day. She seemed to understand that the art dealer and Mike's murderer were likely one and the same, and she wished us a solemn "good luck" as we headed out.

Thoughts of the art meet-up distracted me all day at the farm. The stress of the looming meeting gnawed at my stomach so bad I could barely focus on selling Christmas cookies in the bake shop. Aside from a few stragglers lured in by KP's two-for-one deal, the shop was slow, so that was a blessing. But it's not fun to be lost in your thoughts for long periods of time, and it can be so hard to get out of that trap once you're in it.

The worst part was that I thought I'd left these 'anxious Chelsea' vibes in the past. But I tried not to scold myself too much for feeling a little caught up. Personal growth is not a linear process, and a meeting with a murderer is a better reason than most for backsliding a bit.

Wayne charged into the bakeshop just before closing with a dramatic sigh. I shoved the napkin I'd been doodling on into my pocket and stood straight.

"Hey! Didn't expect to see you here."

He leaned over the counter and gave me a kiss on the cheek. "Can I get an apple cider?"

"Coming right up."

He groaned as he sat at a café table. I furrowed my brow as I walked over to him with the fresh cup of hot, cinnamon-y cider. "You alright?"

He took a big sip of the cider with his eyes closed. "This is the absolute best drink in the world. It's almost syrupy, but it's not too sweet. And the cinnamon and nutmeg... How do you guys do it?"

"If I told you, I'd have to kill you. And honestly, I don't think I have time for that." I sat across from him and sipped from his cup. "What's going on?"

"You're not going to like this."

My chest warmed a few degrees and a dull pain spread into my ribs. Doing my best to keep my mind from wandering to worst case scenarios – another dead body, the wedding has to be cancelled, someone is sick – I kept my mouth shut and waited for more.

"I just got off the phone with Kayla," said Wayne. "She struck out with florists today."

"Is that it?" I said. "You had me scared. I thought it was going to be something bad."

"No flowers at your wedding is no big deal to you?" said Wayne, chuckling to himself. "Why are you so unlike every other woman I've ever met?"

I tried to smile and accept the compliment. The truth was, any other time I think I might have been concerned about the flowers, at least a tiny bit. But I had all that anxious energy coursing through my body. And I couldn't stop thinking about the art thief who might have murdered my ex.

36

THE ART OF DECEPTION

"*I*'m sorry. Excuse me?"

The first thing I noticed about the woman who'd tapped on my shoulder was her big, brown eyes. Her lashes looked like ski-jumps. The smoky makeup on her lids looked as though it had been applied in the green room before *The Tonight Show*. There was an uncommon playfulness in her gaze that matched her bright smile and blonde ponytail.

I thought I recognized her from somewhere, but I couldn't place her. Stepping aside from the milk and sugar area at *The Brown Cow*, I gestured for her to do her thing.

"Sorry," I said. "I take forever to add sugar and cream to my drink. Am I in your way?"

"No, no, no," said the woman. "I'm being so rude. I'm sorry. My name is Jenny. We never met. I just know you from Mike's old Instagram posts. You're Chelsea Thomas, right?"

"Oh! Jealous..." I stopped myself before I said 'Jealous Jenny' in its entirety. "I'm so jealous of your eye makeup. It's so gorgeous. Nice to officially meet you, Jenny."

Miss May and Teeny watched the interaction from their

table across the coffee shop. When I glanced over at them, they didn't even bother looking away. Then, when I looked back to Jenny, I toppled the sugar over, so it spilled all over the coffee bar.

"Oh man," I said. "I was almost at seven full days without an accident. Now I'll have to set the counter back to zero."

Jenny laughed. "You're really funny." She pulled the trash can over and I brushed the spilled sugar inside. "Do you maybe want to join me for a bit at my table? This might be weird, but I've always wondered about you. The girl Mike dated after me."

I looked back over at Teeny and Miss May. Did I want them to get me out of the situation? Maybe for a split-second. But I was interested in talking to Jenny for my own reasons – not the least of which was murder-related – so I followed her to her table, resolving to make the most of the conversation.

"What are you drinking?" Jenny pulled out a chair for me, then sat across from it.

"Peppermint mocha," I said. "It's my Christmas drink. But that's only because it's only available during the holidays. Otherwise, it would be my daily driver."

"Cheers to that." Jenny clinked her cup with mine. "Peppermint mocha for me, too. Extra whipped cream. Looks like we share taste in more than just men."

"Mike wasn't really to my taste," I said. "I mean, may he rest in peace. But, looking back, we weren't a match."

"You're glad he left you at the altar then?" Jenny said it in a way that felt totally non-judgmental and didn't bring up any bad feelings from the past.

"I would have preferred to end the relationship in a less public way. But yeah. We were not supposed to be together."

"Want to know how he and I ended things?" Jenny said.

I indicated for her to carry on, sipping my drink and making eye-contact.

"He dumped me because I didn't want to move to India with him. Like... what? As you can see, I am not Indian."

"I never heard that," I said. "Mike just said –"

"That I was terrible? Angry? Stole his money? Never appreciated him? Oh! Did he say I was jealous? I heard that from a mutual friend a few months after we ended."

Jenny sounded more annoyed with each word she spoke. But I, more than anyone, understood her anger. Mike had a way of drumming that up in people, even from the other side of life. My mind flashed to an image of her bashing him over the head and leaving him for dead in his study. But what fresh motive would Jenny have had in his murder? Why would she have waited years and years? And why would she be around town so much if she'd done it?

"What are you doing here?" I asked. "I mean, Pine Grove is nice, but..."

"I live out in California now, near Berkeley. Flew all the way out for Mike's memorial. Spending a few days with my family over in Blue Mountain. My mom's 70th is coming up and I'm not out this way often, so I figured—"

"Right," I nodded. "You knew Mike from high school."

"Correct," she said. "Go Blue Mountain Badgers." She smiled and looked down. "We didn't date until after college. But we first met in 8th grade biology. He was different back then."

"More acne?"

"More heart," said Jenny. "Less influenced by a desire to make his parents 'proud', whatever that means. Personally, I try to avoid pride. It's not a healthy emotion. Now Mike's gone. And that's kind of what I wanted to talk to you about..." She played with a sugar wrapper, focusing on it like it was the most important thing in the world. "Mike was crummy to me. And everyone knows he was crummy to you. But... Do you feel... Now that he's gone, do you feel bad? Suddenly, it's like I miss him. I miss the good times we had. Never in a million years did I think I'd be so broken up over something like this."

She looked up. I let out a long, slow breath, and looked down into myself, trying to find the truth. "When I first saw him lying there, all sorts of emotions hit me," I said. "Sadness, grief, anger, resentment, fear, anxiety. All that stuff keeps bubbling up in me. But I've been too busy trying to catch Mike's killer to focus on any of it."

"So you're sleeping OK?"

"Weird dreams," I said. "Other than that, I'm alright."

"It's so strange to lose someone you loved a long time ago," said Jenny. "I mean... Maybe neither of us ever truly loved him. But still, it's hard to let go of that hope for closure, you know? Neither of us will ever get that with Mike now."

"I'm hoping finding his killer will do something for me," I said. "But I know exactly what you mean."

37

ART SNOBS

M iss May, Teeny, and I finished up at the *Brown Cow* and walked the short distance to Caputo Park, where we were scheduled to meet the mysterious art dealer. We tittered with nervous excitement on the way there. But when we arrived in the park... No art dealer was there to meet us. We waited. And waited. But no one showed.

"Are you sure we're in the right place, Chelsea?" said Miss May.

I checked the note from Mrs. Vanderhoot for the third time. "Yes. The art dealer was supposed to meet us here ten minutes ago."

"Where is this person then?" said Teeny.

I looked around. From our hiding spot behind a row of bushes, no top-secret art dealers were in our midst, though we had been joined by quite the ominous vibe. Clouds darkened the sun overhead. Tall oak trees swayed in the cold, December wind. A trio of broken candy canes lay at my feet, as though dropped in a Christmas mugging that had happened under the cover of night.

"There!" Miss May pointed through a gap in the bushes where someone approached the park from the street. They wore a black peacoat and black boots and walked with long, confident strides. The individual's back was to us, but somehow, they still felt familiar to me.

"Why aren't they carrying the art?" said Teeny. "It's a sting! Run!"

Miss May clamped her hand down on Teeny's arm. "There's no way they want to do a transaction like this out in the open. This is just a meeting to build trust. If they like us, they'll lead us to the Rembrandt."

"But we don't want the Rembrandt," said Teeny.

"I was speaking hypothetically."

The suspected art thief stopped walking and sat on a bench about midway through the park. Their face was turned away from us, but I nonetheless had a sudden realization. "You're not going to believe this."

"What?" said Miss May.

"I think that's Mike's ex. Jenny."

"What?" said Teeny. "Are you sure?"

"Just follow me." I parted the bushes and stepped out into Caputo Park's main quad. The frozen grass crunched beneath my feet.

Jenny saw me approaching and stood up. "Hi again! Out for a little walk in the park?" She reached out and shook Miss May and Teeny's hands, introducing herself.

They mumbled their own names, looking over at me in disbelief, as if to say, 'Are you sure this girl is the art thief?' I swallowed hard. Less than an hour before, I'd been having a nice chat with this woman. She hadn't seemed like a killer at all. But there was no reason for her to be in the park unless she was the art dealer. If Jenny had killed Mike, that meant she was an extremely dangerous person. Especially since we had her surrounded, and she had everything to lose.

"Well, great to see you again," said Jenny, trying to cut off any potential conversation before it got started. "Enjoy your walk." She cast a look over each shoulder, presumably looking for her mystery 'art buyer,' and eager to get us out of the way before the deal got done. "Bye now."

Jenny smiled, but her clenched fists and tightened jaw belied the anxiety she felt inside. I took a step back. We were standing across from a confirmed art thief and a suspected killer, and she was beginning to take the posture of an animal trapped.

Had Jenny figured out the art deal was a sting? Was she about to run? I looked to Miss May with an imploring look. I didn't know what to do next, and she needed to take the lead.

"I think you know we're not going anywhere," said Miss May in a firm and self-assured voice. "Why don't you sit back down on that bench and talk to us?"

Jenny's nostrils flared. "What are you talking about?"

"I'm talking about your body language," said Miss May. "When you first saw us, you were relaxed. At that point, you genuinely thought you were running into some kindly townsfolk you'd just seen at the coffee shop. Then you got nervous, like your buyer might show up any second. A few seconds passed and you clenched up, like you were ready for a fight. That's when I knew you had this whole situation figured out."

Miss May, ladies and gentleman. Always showing up her co-sleuths. Never afraid of a confrontation.

"Keen observations," said Teeny, stepping forward. "I concur."

Jenny stammered, taking a step backward. Just looking

at her, I was sure her heart was racing, her mind was going even faster than her heart, and she was willing to do anything to escape us without going to jail.

Her face reddened. Her pupils grew two sizes as she looked from me, to Teeny, to Miss May. "I didn't kill anyone."

"No one said you did," said Miss May. "Now why don't you sit on the bench, and we'll talk."

Jenny stumbled two more steps backwards. "No! I don't have to talk to you."

"You stole the Rembrandt from Mike's safe," said Miss May. "We already have that confirmed."

"I didn't kill anyone!"

"And we believe you," said Miss May, looking over at me and Teeny. "Isn't that right?"

Uh... No. "Yup. We believe you."

My tone must not have been convincing, because Jenny's reply came fast. "He was already dead when I got there."

"So you went there to steal his art, and it just so happened he'd been murdered earlier in the night?" said Miss May.

Jenny shook her head. A tear streamed down her cheek. "I went there to talk to him. That's all. He hadn't paid child support since she was born. My baby needs food. My baby needs clothes. And he owed it to us."

"Hold up. You and Mike had a baby?" I asked.

Jenny nodded. "I went there to ask for the money. And I was mad, I can admit that. I didn't care if his girlfriend was home or anything, I was going to tell her all about us. But then I showed up and he was... He was just laying there. There was no way I was going to get my money from a dead man. I knew the combination to the safe. Had to take my chance."

I looked away, my perception of Mike changing for what

felt like the twentieth time in my life. The whole time we'd
been together, he'd said he wanted to wait until he was at
least 40 years old before he had a kid of his own. Then he
went and got Jenny pregnant, and refused to pay child
support. Um, what?

The more I found out about Mike, the more I wondered
how I'd missed so many red flags, and the more gratitude
filled my body. I was so lucky Mike had left me at the altar
that day. I'd gotten so much stronger since then, and he'd
spared me the unfortunate fate that had befallen both
Priscilla and Jenny.

"I can't believe Mike was a dad," I said.

"Barely," said Jenny, blowing her nose. "So what
happens now? Are you going to take me to jail or something? I'll go. I know stealing is wrong. Obviously. And I
wouldn't want to set that example for Bonnie. But..." Her
chin quivered. "She needs me."

Miss May looked Jenny up and down, her eyes crinkling
with compassion. "As far as I'm concerned, we're looking for
a killer, not an art thief."

"My sediment exactly," said Teeny.

"Sentiment," I said, cringing at my own instinct to
correct.

"No. Sediment," said Teeny. "The little crumbs at the
bottom of my mind tell me that Jenny should sell her art to
the highest bidder and ride off into the sunset with her baby
on her hip."

Jenny's face broke out into the first genuine smile I'd
seen from her all day. The smile brightened her eyes,
revealing little crow's feet I hadn't noticed before. *I bet those
crow's feet developed from too many nights spent crying*, I
thought. *Hopefully now Jenny's luck will change.*

"Thank you so much," she said. "You won't regret this."

38

OFF ROAD RAGE

*B*y the time we got back to *Grandma's* it was lunch time, and the carolers were still there. They sang a slow, ominous version of "Hark Hear the Bells,"and the suspenseful energy of the song carried over into every aspect of the world around me.

I cautiously stepped into the restaurant, my heart aching with unease. It was just before the lunch rush, so the joyful atmosphere that usually engulfed the place during the Christmas season was absent. The twinkling lights and joyful decorations somehow lost their luster, as if overshadowed by the unseen darkness of the murderer at large.

Teeny and Miss May followed close behind me, their expressions mirroring my own unease. They'd both been on the phone handling business on our walk over from the park, so we hadn't yet talked about our conversation with

Jenny. But as I got settled at our booth, I felt more and more unsure.

Jenny was in the winter wind, and I hadn't been fully convinced of her innocence.

Teeny hurried off to the kitchen to deal with whatever she'd been talking on the phone about. Miss May wrapped up her call with KP (which seemed to mostly concern his desire to sell more trees). The absence of familiar faces made the restaurant feel hauntingly empty. The tables, usually filled with laughter and warmth, stood as silent witnesses to the unsettling atmosphere.

Sure, there was a table of three eating quietly in the far corner. And an elderly man ate soup and read the paper at a table nearby. But I felt more and more alone as I sat there waiting for Teeny and Miss May to be ready to talk. More and more, I felt the presence of the killer lurking in Pine Grove.

The scent of Teeny's Santa Squash wafted through the air, its comforting aroma juxtaposed against the looming sense of danger. My hands trembled involuntarily as I reached out to touch the familiar table before me. The surface felt cold, almost lifeless, as if absorbing the heaviness that ran through my body.

Finally, Miss May ended her phone call and looked at me with a smile, and my little bubble of mystery and suspense popped. Colors were brighter. Sounds were crisper. A happy family bustled through the front door, laughing.

"Remind me to fire KP whenever I stop loving him more than pretty much anyone on earth," said Miss May.

"Careful talking like that," I said. "John Wentworth might start to get jealous."

Miss May chuckled. "John's too busy eating coconut shrimp in Key West to be jealous of anyone or anything. And if you imply that KP and I have some kind of romantic connection ever again, I'm going to be sick all over this nice restaurant." She craned her neck around. "Where's Teeny?"

"Work stuff," I said.

"Let's get down to business then," said Miss May. "I'm not convinced Jenny didn't kill Mike."

I felt the color drain from my face. "What?"

"She didn't give us any concrete evidence of her innocence," said Miss May. "In fact, she provided a motive for the murder, and placed herself in Mike's house pretty much at the exact moment he died. Oh. And she outed herself as a thief."

"But we let her go."

"We let her go because if she is guilty, she's going to incriminate herself very, very soon. And that's way easier than bringing her in without any real proof that she killed him."

"Why do you think she's so eager to incriminate herself?"

"The woman is desperate," said Miss May. "She met us in broad daylight, in Pine Grove, hoping to sell a stolen piece of art. You don't do that if you're thinking straight. You do that if you need money for a getaway car, or a getaway life. I'm not sold on the baby story, either. Mike seem like a dad to you?"

"Not really," I said.

"Look, he was a crummy guy, we both know that. That notwithstanding, he never struck me as the type to flake on a responsibility like that. If anything, he would have paid Jenny extra just to keep her from telling Priscilla about the kid. Priscilla clearly had no idea about the baby, so Mike was either paying Jenny, or the kid doesn't really exist."

. . .

"So now what? We go to Jenny's house? We follow her around town? I don't even know where she lives."

"Eduardo hacked her account on the art sales site and got me her home address," said Miss May. "It pays to have a social media intern."

"That's not social media," I said. "That's corrupting the youth of America for your own personal gain."

"I'm giving the kid an integral role in catching a killer running rampant in his cute-as-a-snowman's-button hometown. That's hardly corruption, Chels."

The carolers came inside, singing "Rockin' Around the Christmas Tree" at top volume. Miss May clapped along, bobbing her head. As she mouthed the words (getting most of them wrong), I sat back in wonder.

Miss May was so calm, cool, and relaxed. She'd developed a plan, seemingly while talking to KP on the phone. And she seemed unfazed by the task that lay ahead. Sure, she might have been a bit nervous if she knew what we'd find on the way to Jenny's place. But she was living in the moment, which is sometimes the most you can do in a town with as many murders as Pine Grove.

.   .   .

That night, I was abruptly awakened by blaring sirens, their shrill cries piercing through the stillness of the night. Curiosity gripped me, and I got dressed, slipping into my cozy coat and grabbing my car keys. Miss May was already out on the porch when I got downstairs, and she followed me wordlessly out to my car.

We spoke little as I followed the row of ambulances, their sirens guiding my path through the pitch-black night. I tried Wayne, but his phone went straight to voicemail, so all the information we had came from the emergency vehicles before us, leading us into the unknown.

As I drove, a sense of anticipation hung in the air, heightening my senses. "They're headed down to the river," I said. "Something must have happened on the Blue Mountain Bridge."

Miss May made no response other than a small nod.

An image of the Blue Mountain Bridge filled my mind. It connected one side of the Hudson River to the next, and it was famous for its sloping design and quiet elegance. There had been tragedies on the bridge before, and I prayed another did not await us that night.

.   .   .

The rhythmic hum of my engine provided my only sense of comfort as we got closer to the bridge. Vvvvvv. Vvvvvvvv. Vvvvvvvvvvvv. I focused on the sounds within the sound in order to keep my mind from wandering away. The growl was built like a Russian Doll and, listening carefully, I could pick out several decibels working at once.

Finally, I came to a stop behind the row of ambulances in the center of the bridge, and I could see the source of commotion. A car had crashed through the guardrail and plummeted into the river, headfirst. Its headlights cast an eerie glow in the water below, lending an ethereal quality to the scene. The sight sent a shiver down my spine.

I didn't know it then, but it was a significant moment in the murder of the evil ex-boyfriend, and a step closer to the truth.

BRIDGE OVER TROUBLED WATER

I spotted Wayne, peering over the broken guardrail, and hurried over to him. "Wayne…"

He sighed. "Driver went over. County's got divers down there now."

"The county? Really?"

"Middle of the bridge. The county is involved, we're involved, the town across the river is involved. It's a mess."

"Have they found anything?"

"Driver's missing. Swept away by the current, probably."

"And whose car is it?"

Wayne cast a look over his shoulder. Chief Sunshine Flanagan was a good distance away, looking distracted, and, honestly, a little bored.

"I shouldn't tell you this."

"Come on, Wayne," I said. "Something's going on with Flanagan. You're already getting locked out of the murder investigation. If this is related…"

"Fine." He looked over at Flanagan once more, then back to me. "The driver's name is Jenny Carlson. Apparently, she and Mike used to date."

INSANE INVITATION

I looked down at the Hudson, illuminated by police lights from every angle. Had I not been told, I'd have no idea a car had plunged into the river less than an hour prior. The water's surface was occasionally broken by a diver returning from the depths below. Other than that, all was still.

Police walkies squawked every so-often in the distance. Somewhere that felt thousands of miles away, I heard someone ask if there was any coffee. Yellow police tape fluttered noiselessly in the breeze.

"What do you mean you knew her?" said Wayne.

I told him all about what had happened with Jenny earlier that day, starting at the coffee shop and working my way gradually toward that very moment on the bridge. He rubbed his temple, shaking his head. "Why didn't you call me?"

"We were going to find stronger evidence of her guilt," I said. "I guess I thought we'd see it through before plugging you in."

His chest heaved as he breathed in deep then let it out.

One foot at a time, he climbed up on the guardrail, then peered over. "Doubt there was anything we could have done, anyway."

"You could have locked her up for art theft," I said. "If she were in jail, she never would have driven over the edge of this bridge."

Miss May spoke up from behind me. "Do you think she drove off, or do you think she was driven off?"

Wayne and Miss May greeted one another with solemn head nods.

"I hadn't considered that she might have been forced off the road." I turned to Wayne. "I haven't looked, are there tire tracks on the bridge? Any sign that she might have been trying to get away from someone, or avoid this fate?"

"She didn't even tap her brakes," said Wayne. "It's like she was determined to do this. If everything you said is true... I mean, I don't want to say this, but..."

"You don't think this was an accident," said Miss May. "You think the girl had too many problems, and she saw this as her only viable solution."

"Just saying it's a possibility."

"What about her kid, Bonnie?" I asked. "Have you been able to determine if Jenny was in the car alone?"

"County said Jenny's body is missing. Probably got pulled down to the bottom somehow. But they got to the car before it sank and no one mentioned a car seat. Those things stay locked in pretty much no matter what. Doubtful there was a kid in there with her."

"Oh, thank goodness." Miss May clutched her heart. "What happens now?"

Down below, a diver surfaced, pulled his mask off, and ran a hand through his hair. Wayne called down to him. "Anything?"

The diver shook his head. "Car's too far down. It's too dark. We gotta call it."

Wayne motioned for Flanagan to approach. "Chief. You wanna come handle this?"

Flanagan was glued to the same spot she'd been in when we'd arrived, looking off into the distance. She didn't budge when Wayne called her name. "Hey Chief!"

When she didn't respond again, Wayne charged over to her in several loud, annoyed steps. I couldn't hear what he said to her, but he looked frustrated, and she looked comatose. Eventually, she nodded along with what he was saying, but even then, her demeanor was detached and apathetic.

Wayne hurried back to get things settled with the diver and made arrangements with the additional county and local cops, but I kept my focus on Flanagan.

"Something is up with her," I said to Miss May.

"I know," said Miss May. "The woman has always been a thorn in our side. Honestly, she's bothered me more times than I can count. But this is worse. Now it seems like she doesn't even care."

"Do you think she's given up on keeping Pine Grove safe? Our murder rate per capita must be higher than most small towns in the area. Maybe she's zoning out 'cuz she knows we'll beat her to the punch anyway."

"I doubt that." Miss May narrowed her eyes, still looking in Flanagan's direction. "Why don't we go talk to her? See what's up?"

I was about to protest when Miss May crossed over toward Flanagan. Unsure what to do with myself, I followed. What happened next shocked me.

"You know there's a car in the river there, Chief," said Miss May.

Up close, I noticed that the circles under Flanagan's eyes had darkened considerably. Her temples were dotted with acne. Matted and unkempt, her hair was far from its typical glory. And was that a slight paunch sitting atop her washboard abs?

"You knew this person? Jenny?" Flanagan's voice was scratchy.

"We'll get to that," said Miss May. "But you've got to tell us what in the name of all things fried and crispy is going on with you. Because we both know I've never been your biggest fan, but you're not acting like yourself, and I don't like it. We need you back, Chief."

Emotion sprung to Flanagan's face. She looked away.

Miss May took a step closer. "You can talk to us."

There was a long pause. When Flanagan spoke again, her voice was strained and wobbly. It was the sound of a woman trying not to cry. Personally, I'd never sounded like that, because we all know I cried liberally back in the day. But my heart filled with pity when I heard the pain in her voice.

"I... I don't... I don't want to talk about it."

"OK." Miss May exhaled through her nose. "But there is something going on?"

Flanagan gave Miss May a small nod, looking down at the ground with intense focus. I don't know what came over me, but I wanted nothing more than to help her feel better.

"Are you busy tomorrow night?" I said.

"Why?" Flanagan looked up at me with big, bloodshot eyes.

"Because Wayne and I are having our rehearsal dinner. And I want you to come."

41

DARLING D'AVOLA'S

"*W*e're taking the next two days off from the investigation," said Miss May, scrubbing at the kitchen counter.

"We just had a suspect drive off a bridge." I threw up my hands and grabbed a rag, scrubbing at the counter a little ways down from where she was working.

"And that's exactly why we're taking a couple days off," she said. "It's your wedding day. I don't want you thinking about people getting murdered or catapulting to their watery graves. Does any of that sound romantic to you?"

"I'm not a sicko," I said. "But you know what else doesn't sound romantic to me? Another dead body shows up. We get word of it just before the ceremony is about to begin. And we could have prevented the murder if only we'd focused on solving the mystery the day before."

"Whoever killed Mike has shown no interest in committing a second murder."

"Unless that same person forced Jenny off the road." I raised my eyebrows at Miss May. "Admit it. It's a distinct possibility."

"That doesn't fit the profile of this killer one tiny bit," said Miss May. "This is a person who bashed Mike's head in with –"

"Let's not get into the gory details, please."

"I'm just saying, this killer isn't afraid to get up close and personal," said Miss May. "Bumping someone off the road and into the river is about the least personal way to kill someone I can imagine."

"It's not less personal than hiring a hitman," I said.

"Do you think you're going to win something one day for pointing out the tiny flaws in other people's thinking?"

"Do you?" I smirked.

Miss May chuckled. "We can share the prize. Now go do whatever brides do the day before their wedding. I have a rehearsal dinner to plan, and if you don't get out of my way, I'm going to physically remove you from my kitchen. *D'Avola's* at 6. Don't be late."

I scoffed. "Like I'd be late for my own rehearsal dinner." Miss May gave me a stern look. I hung my head. "Fine, fine. I'll be on time."

"Cuz I'm not driving you. Remember?"

"I remember. You're going to be there early, and Wayne is picking his parents up from the Bronx and meeting us at six. I need to get myself there and I need to get myself there on time."

Miss May gave me a hug and she kissed me on the top of the head. "Don't hate me for nagging you."

"Don't hate me if I'm late."

Miss May laughed and shoved me out of the kitchen, muttering threats as I stumbled out, giggling right along with her.

I spent the day painting my toenails, answering congrat- ulations texts from old friends, and generally reveling in the calm before the wedding. *A Christmas Story* was on TV as I did my hair and got dressed for the night, and I recited the lines along with the characters without needing to look at the TV to get them right.

Most of my favorite quotes ("You used up all the glue on purpose!" "I can't put my arms down!") were from Randy. But my favorite line in the movie came from its narrator, Ralphie. Every time I hear it, I crack up laughing, and I hear it at least five times every holiday season.

"Only I didn't say 'fudge.' I said the word, the big one, the queen-mother of dirty words!"

Anyway. I digress. The good news is that even with the distraction of Ralphie and his group of misfit friends, I was dressed and ready a full hour before the rehearsal dinner was set to begin, so I pulled my puffy coat on over my red and green dress and headed over to *D'Avola's* to check it out.

I know what you're thinking. Why didn't I have my rehearsal dinner at *Grandma's*? Trust me, Teeny practically begged me to let her host. But that lady is such a huge part of my life. I wanted her to be able to be fully present for every second of the rehearsal and the wedding. Besides, there's something extra-charming about rehearsal dinner at your favorite pizza place on Christmas Eve, don't you think?

Rita D'Avola welcomed me with a big hug and a kiss on the cheek. She had little Vinnie in her arms. They were wearing matching red sweaters. I had to take a selfie with them as soon as I entered.

"What are you doing here so early?" said Rita, brushing her hair from her face.

"One, two, three!" I snapped the picture and stepped away, shoving the phone back in my purse. "Can't a girl be early to her own rehearsal dinner?"

"Of course, she can," said Rita. "It's just, Miss May said to expect you at least thirty minutes late."

"This place looks incredible, Rita." I beamed as I looked around. Market lights were strung across the ceiling. Checkered table clothes were laid out on every table, each of which had a dozen tea lights dotting its surface. Tom Gigley and *The Giggles* rehearsed quiet, jazzy versions of Christmas tunes, set up in the corner of the restaurant. And the place smelled like pizza, pasta, and fresh-baked bread. It was all so charming I thought I might explode.

The next hour passed quickly as I greeted early-birds and helped Miss May, Teeny and Rita with the finishing touches at the restaurant. Just when I realized Wayne hadn't yet arrived, I heard him call my name from over near the door.

I looked and there stood my almost husband, handsome as ever, in a navy suit with a red tie. He was standing with his parents, and they all three wore identical, adorable little smiles.

I'd met Wayne's parents once or twice over the past year, but every time I saw them was just as exciting as the first. The two of them could not have been sweeter. Wayne's mom was five-foot-nothing, with a thick Bronx accent and a forceful, loving hug to match. His dad was the quieter of the two, balding, also on the shorter side. He had a patient, kind demeanor, and the kindest eyes I think I've ever seen.

"You look gorgeous, as always." Wayne's dad kissed me on the cheek.

"Alright, Al, stop flirting with the bride to be." His mom nudged his dad away and wrapped me up in a big hug. "Ready for tomorrow?"

"Absolutely."

As the evening progressed, toasts and laughter intermingled with heartfelt wishes of love and support, and the magic of the evening permeated every corner of the restaurant. Everything was so special, part of me wished we would have gotten married and celebrated the whole wedding at *D'Avola's* that night. Though if that were the case, I wouldn't have gotten to live the most exciting wedding day in the history of Pine Grove. But we'll get to that later.

I ran into Flanagan toward the end of the party, as I rushed off to the bathroom to touch up my makeup. She was standing over by the coat rack, still wearing her jacket, looking unsure if she should stay or go.

"Chief! Hi! Are you leaving already? I didn't see you in there." I had hugged so many people that night that I hugged Flanagan without thinking. She hugged me back, then pushed a small, silver gift bag into my arms.

"That's for you and Wayne."

"Oh. Wow. Thank you."

"I'm not leaving," she said, her voice stilted and odd. "Actually, um, I... I just got here. I'm sorry I'm late."

"Better you than me." I smiled. "Let me hang up your coat for you."

Flanagan slipped out of her coat. There was that vacant look in her eyes again. "You OK?"

She nodded. "Yeah. But maybe... After the party... Could I speak with you and Wayne?"

42

AIN'T NO SUNSHINE

*T*he party dwindled to a slow close, as only the best tend to do. Rita D'Avola ended up singing alongside Tom Gigley, belting out renditions of "Silent Night" and "Jingle Bell Rock" at the top of her lungs. Teeny danced circles around Big Dan, who nodded his head ever-so-slightly in time with the music. Miss May and John Wentworth laughed over big, cheesy slices of pizza, John wearing a brand-new Hawaiian shirt he'd picked up in Key West.

One by one, every member of the wedding party (small on my side but rich with chummy groomsmen from Wayne's policing past), hugged me goodbye and headed out into the night, which hopefully had been warmed by the generous pours of whiskey and wine at the bar.

Wayne and I were the last to leave. It had been a while, and there had been so much excitement, I'd forgotten about my strange interaction with Flanagan. She was waiting out in the parking lot, leaning against a lamppost and scrolling through her phone. The phone disappeared into her back pocket as Wayne and I approached.

I slipped my arm into the crook of his elbow. Speaking

out of the side of his mouth, he said, "You have no idea what this is about?"

We were so close to Flanagan at that point, the only communication tool available to me was a slight shake of the head. Wayne replied with a slight tensing of the arm. Flanagan gave us a disheartened smile as we closed within a few feet.

"How was the dinner?"

"It was great. Good food." Wayne said. I knew from his body language that he wasn't in any place to tolerate small talk, so the fact that he said as much as he did impressed me. Yes, it was only those five words, but my man is not what one might call the 'verbal type.' "Now can we talk about what's going on here? You've got me a little freaked out, Chief."

Her smile faded. "It's nothing like that." Flanagan ran a hand through her hair. She'd been looking tired lately, but over the course of that day the fatigue had turned a corner. No longer did the tiredness detract from her natural beauty. Instead, the dark circles and sunken cheeks, in that parking lot light, brought out perfect bone structure and annoyingly pretty eyes.

"What's it like then?" said Wayne.

Flanagan took a deep breath in, then exhaled. "I'm sorry."

My eyes widened. She let the apology sit there for a moment. It was like hot bread that had just been dropped on the table at a fancy restaurant. There was a sense that we all wanted to touch it, but no one was willing to go first.

"I've been rude to you both since I arrived in Pine Grove," she continued. "Chelsea, I got in the way of your investigations. Wayne, I gave you a hard time at the precinct. I was obnoxious, as a general matter, and I'd like to explain."

Wayne glanced over at me before returning his gaze to Flanagan. "Do you want to go back inside or something?"

"I want to do this in the cold." Flanagan straightened her shoulders and stood tall. "There are no excuses for the way I've behaved, and I take full responsibility for all of it. That said, as I'm sure you've both learned in your investigations, there are always reasons we do the things we do."

I nodded. Even though Flanagan was apologizing, she gave me that "called to the principal's office" feeling, and my stomach was tied up in a sailor's knot. I'll tell you, by the end of the conversation, I'd come to understand Flanagan better than I ever thought I would, but at that point, I had no idea such understanding was on the horizon.

"I don't know if you know this, but before I took this job, I'd spent a few years working as a private investigator down on the Jersey Shore. P.I. work was a welcome break after years of dealing with the bureaucracy of policing. And I was in a tiny town, where nothing bad ever happened, so the work was simple."

"I used to live in a town like that," I said, thinking back to what Pine Grove was like before the murders.

"Right." Flanagan let out another sigh. "I'm telling you, my first dozen or cases were so simple, they almost bored me. Six missing cats were located. One local judge was caught playing penny slots with town money. Stuff like that. That's why I didn't expect it when... When... When Scott..."

Wayne leaned forward. "Scott? Who's Scott? What happened?" I put a hand on his arm, and he backed off a bit. "Sorry."

Flanagan sniffled. "Scott was my husband. He was murdered, and I failed to solve the case."

"Whoa." I covered my mouth, which had suddenly gotten quite dry. "I'm so sorry."

A tragic smile flickered across Flanagan's face. The smile was heavy with loss and nostalgia, weighed down by the pain behind her eyes. "When I met you, Chelsea, you were all worked up about being left at the altar. Everyone was talking like nothing worse had ever happened to a woman. I was fresh off what had happened with Scott. I guess it just... hit me wrong. My pain was so real... so fresh... So much more violent, you know? You became my enemy in my mind."

I took a step back. My muscles tensed. Sunshine Flanagan had suddenly become human to me. But humans are capable of all sorts of evil. Had she killed Mike and framed me to settle some kind of invisible score?

"What are you saying, Chief?" Wayne clutched my arm tight. He must have been thinking the same thing.

"I didn't kill anyone." Flanagan looked off to the side and shook her head. "Far from it. I've spent the better part of this year trying to think of ways to make up for the way I've treated you both, and for the way I've failed this town."

"You would have solved those mysteries if Pine Grove wasn't blessed with so many incredible sleuths," said Wayne. "That's how I console myself, at least."

"The reason I failed to solve the murders in Pine Grove was because of that regional supervisor, Tate," said Flanagan. "He's had me hog tied since the moment I arrived in town. Everything I want to do requires paperwork, and convincing, and more paperwork. Why do you think you're always bogged down in busy work, Wayne?"

"Me and the guys assumed it was because you hate us," said Wayne.

"I don't hate any of you," said Flanagan, a sliver of light returning to her eyes. "But I've realized I can't stay in Pine Grove anymore."

"Why not?" said Wayne.

"I have a sick aunt back in my hometown. And there's a mystery waiting for me there, that I only I can solve."

"...Scott." I said it so quietly, I don't think Flanagan heard me.

"I put in my two weeks with King Tate earlier today. Once the new year comes around, I'll be headed out."

"This is all...kind of sad and kind of heartwarming and kind of tragic," I said. "I'm glad you told us. But why tonight?"

"I guess I thought that me leaving might feel kind of like a wedding present for the two of you," said Flanagan. "Also, once you're married... I was wondering..."

I narrowed my eyes. What could Flanagan possibly say next?

"I'd like to help you find Michael Gherkin's killer. If you'll have me."

43

SUNSHINE RISES

*W*e stayed out in that parking lot for an hour, running Flanagan through every detail of the case thus far. We all agreed that the killer had an obvious familiarity with Mike's life. They knew about my history with Mike, and chances were decent they wanted to take us both down with a single murder.

Flanagan had explored the connections surrounding Mike's business partners, his ex-best friend and Priscilla's crime-addled family. Like us, she'd found nothing.

It's astounding, really, how hard it is to solve a crime. Back when I was a kid reading mystery novels, things seemed so much more straightforward. There were red herrings, sure, but nine times out of ten, I solved the murder before the murderer was revealed.

In real life, the whole endeavor is far more challenging. Suddenly it's just you and your friends against an unknown killer, who could be literally any person on the face of the earth. Miss May, Teeny, and I work to narrow things down, and that technique has proven successful. But you never know how close you are, and until the lights are turned on, you're feeling around blindly in the dark.

Talking to Flanagan, I realized that the process is just as unclear for the police. To a certain extent, I knew that already, thanks to talking with Wayne. Still, I imagined that higher up the ladder, the cops had special technology that would help them see into that darkness better than the common person.

Not true. In the case of the Pine Grove Police Department, there is no technology to help. And the regional supervisor is so pig-headed and strict with regulations, in many ways the cops have serious disadvantages in the world of solving murders.

Cops are just regular people. With training, and guns, and lots and lots of red-tape.

Eventually, the three of us worked our way around to Jenny and her sunken car. No surprise, Pine Grove did not have the funds to recover the vehicle from the bottom of the Hudson. (What's the carbon footprint of dumping an entire car into a river?) But Flanagan shared one valuable piece of information about Jenny's accident:

Divers managed to do a thorough search of the sunken vehicle (those divers were paid for by the county, by the way), and they did not discover any art in the car. That indicated Jenny had not gone down with the Rembrandt. The painting was most likely out there somewhere, perhaps in the hands of another thief, and it was possible that said thief had forced Jenny off the road, most likely to keep her from retaliation.

At the end of the conversation, Flanagan trained her gorgeous eyes on me. "The way I see it, there's one important question we need to answer before we make any progress here."

Gulp. "What's that?" I said.

"Why are you still alive?" Wayne said to me.

Flanagan nodded. "Exactly. The killer wanted to take you down with Mike. That's why they left that forged note. But you're not in jail yet."

"Maybe they don't hate me that much after all?" I said weakly.

"Or maybe they're furious that I didn't lock you up after reading that note," said Flanagan. I hope this isn't true, but it's possible the killer is waiting in the wings, looking for an opportunity to kill you, too."

A slow dread crept up my throat, slithering like a serpent behind my eyes. My wedding was less than 24 hours away. And someone out there wanted me dead.

44

WEDDING WHOAS

I woke up the morning of my wedding with a weird amount of crust in my eyes. It's not a glamorous detail, I know. But no woman wakes up on her wedding day already perfectly made-up and beautiful. It takes a lot of work! And getting the crust out of your eyes is an important first step in that process.

My chest tingled with excitement as I sat up and dangled my legs off the side of my bed. *This is my wedding day,* I thought. *Tomorrow at this time, I'm going to be Wayne's wife.*

A peaceful smile spread across my face. There's plenty of unrest in the world. Goodness knows, there was a whole lot of unrest in Pine Grove on my wedding day. But I was getting married, for real this time, and that was a good thing.

I walked downstairs to the sounds of Frank Sinatra Christmas music floating up from the kitchen. My peaceful smile expanded into a huge grin as I remembered. It wasn't merely my wedding day. It was Christmas. My favorite day of the year.

Miss May wrapped me up in a huge hug as I shuffled into the kitchen. "There she is! The Christmas bride. Looking well-rested and ready for her big day." She took a step back from me. "Chelsea. I know I've said it before. But I cannot believe you are getting married."

"Because you thought I'd never find a man to love me?" I said.

"Because, to me, you're still the thirteen-year-old girl who moved onto this farm with two suitcases and a scared look in your eyes." Miss May's second hug was tighter than the first, and she held on for longer. "I love you, you know that?"

"I've heard rumors about it," I said. "I love you too."

Miss May gestured toward the kitchen table, where a gorgeous breakfast spread awaited us. Croissants, bagels, eggs, fresh pineapple chunks and champagne flutes filled with mimosas. "Sit, sit. Wedding Day Christmas Breakfast!"

The back door kicked open and Teeny bustled in, yanking off her hat and gloves. "I'm here! I'm here! Sorry I'm late!"

"Late? I don't think I told you to come this morning. Did I?" said Miss May, taking Teeny's coat and hanging it on the rack.

"Suddenly I need to be invited to Wedding Day Christmas Breakfast?" Teeny asked. "That's insane."

"You left Big Dan all alone to come be with me?" I said. "He can come too, if he wants."

"According to Big Dan, all he wants for Christmas is to not have to move," said Teeny. "I told him he's going to be spending all night on the dance floor, but he can be in a coma until then for all I care. He said something about how dancing is the most pointless activity in the world, then I gave him a look, and he said he couldn't wait to dance all night. Then he said 'woo hoo' without smiling or looking me in the eye, so we're good now. Ooo, pancakes!"

Teeny grabbed a pancake with her hands and took a bite, smiling. Just like that, Wedding Day Christmas Breakfast had begun. And so too had the last chapter of one of the most harrowing mysteries we'd investigated yet.

The three of us spent the morning gabbing, exchanging Christmas gifts, and talking about how excited we were for the wedding later. A few times, either Teeny or I slipped up and mentioned the investigation, but whenever that happened Miss May would say "No ex-boyfriend talk on your wedding day. No murder talk on your wedding day. No murdered ex-boyfriend talk on your wedding day," and we'd clam up pretty quick.

In case you're curious, I got Miss May a brand-new set of apple-themed pajamas. And I got Teeny a professional-looking cookbook with all her best recipes, which she absolutely adored. Although I'd demanded that neither Teeny nor Miss May get me anything for Christmas (they'd both done so much for the wedding already), they'd teamed up to buy me a gorgeous set of pans from Le Creuset, which they insisted was a crucial part of any newlywed's cooking arsenal.

The first half of the day moved slowly, like it always does on Christmas, and it felt like forever until it was time for me to get ready for the wedding. Then an automated alarm went off and Miss May jumped up from the game of Scrabble we'd been playing. "Time to get dressed for the big to-do!"

I stood from the game, muttering about how she just didn't want to lose another round to me, but Miss May had already bustled off to her room to get prepped, and Teeny had followed close behind, hoisting her dress bag with all her strength.

I entered my bedroom to find my wedding dress hanging in front of my window, backlit by the soft, December sun. Rays of light streamed through the tulle, so the dress radiated warmth, and its little beads and crystals shimmered gorgeously. I smiled. Miss May had hung my dress up. And she'd left a small envelope on my writing desk.

The envelope said "Dear Chelsea" on the front. I teared up when I saw the handwriting. The letter was not from Miss May. It was from my mother.

Clutching it to my chest, I took a ragged breath in. My parents had been gone for almost twenty years. I'd gotten so used to life without them that they hadn't yet occurred to me all day. Then I found that letter, and I felt like they were with me again.

I opened the envelope slowly, careful not to create any unnecessary rips. The note inside was simple, written in my mother's gorgeous, swooping cursive.

"My Dear Chelsea,

You deserve all of the best things from life. I'll be with you today, and so will your father. We love you and we're so incredibly proud of the woman you've become.

Remember: life isn't always easy, but that's what makes it so much fun.

Love Always,

Mom"

I read the letter three times in a row. Tears streamed down my cheeks. Sitting on my bed, I held it close to my chest again. Gradually, the tears slowed and gave way to my biggest smile of the day. My mother's love had been with me my whole life, even when I hadn't realized it. It always would be, and I was lucky for that.

Slowly, I stood and removed my wedding dress from the hanger. As soon as I touched it, a memory grabbed me by the shoulders and turned me toward the past.

The last time I'd slipped into a wedding dress things had not turned out well. I'd looked nice, I thought. But that hadn't mattered much once Mike had left me all alone at the altar and it had become clear that he was never coming back.

I remembered the way Miss May had looked at me when I was all alone up there. I remembered the shocked look on Mike's mom's face. And, for the first time, I remembered the way his cousin Ryker had snickered at me as I did my 'walk of shame' back down the aisle. My mind couldn't break away from that look on Ryker's face, and a hot, angry warmth built in my stomach.

"What was that guy's problem?" My jaw dropped as I continued speaking. "He'd always hated Mike. And he'd always hated *me*."

45

ALMOST JUST MARRIED

I ran down the hall with my wedding dress bustled in my hand. "Miss May!" In my rush, I slipped on the runner and slammed into Miss May's bedroom door with my shoulder, spilling into the room. It was empty. In three steps, I was inside her walk-in closet. The dress Miss May had picked out for my wedding was gone, as were her heels. And so was she.

The kitchen was empty. Miss May's van was parked outside, but Teeny's pink convertible was gone. I scanned the counter for a note and found one wedged under the fruit basket (which had been piled with Christmas cookies for about a month).

"Ho ho ho! Ran out with Santa for a special, secret errand! See you at the wedding!"

A pebble of fear wiggled its way between my vertebrae. I thought I knew who the killer was, and it seemed I might have to apprehend him all by myself...

My T-bird was parked outside. "Just Married" was written on the back window in big, white letters. Beer cans were tied to the rear. The keys called to me from the peg near the kitchen door.

Keys. Ignition. Seatbelt. Click. Mirrors. Adjusted. Tires. Burning rubber.

I was headed toward the Gherkin home in Blue Mountain with less than an hour left before I had to be back at the farm for my wedding. I know, I know. Miss May had forbidden talking about murdered ex-boyfriends on my wedding day. But she'd said nothing about bringing justice to that dead ex, and I was determined to do just that.

Speeding down the back roads toward Blue Mountain, my mind flashed with thoughts of Wayne. He and his groomsmen were at his place, putting on their tuxes, maybe drinking classy whiskey, getting ready for the big day. Part of me wanted to call him and tell him to meet me at the Gherkin house. But it's bad luck for the groom to see the bride in her dress before they're at the altar. Then there were bridesmaids. My cousin, Maggie. My new friend Aidy. They'd be more than willing to help. But I didn't want to call them. I wanted them to focus on getting ready for the wedding.

Besides, it was important for me to handle this one on my own. No longer was I sweaty, teary-eyed mess who disappeared into a pile of Lo Mein after getting left at the altar. Absolutely not! I was Chelsea Thomas, local sleuth extraordinaire, independent woman, freedom fighter, and lover of all things buttery and baked!

I slammed the radio on with the palm of my hand. A hard-rock version of "Hark Hear the Bells" catapulted from the speakers with sharp guitars, pounding drums and a relentless bass line that beat perfectly in time with my racing heart.

My instinct told me that Ryker Gherkin had killed my

ex. There was no way I was getting married without taking him down. I was too angry to fail. And I knew if I could keep that anger with me, I could defeat anyone in a fight.

But when Ryker opened the door to greet me, casually eating a string cheese, all that anger fizzled into confusion. I stammered, trying to explain why I was there, in my wedding dress. He scratched his head, casually munching, looking more innocent than anyone I'd ever accused.

Then I heard her slippery voice, "Hello, Chelsea," and everything changed.

46

THE GHERK STORE CALLED

*J*enny stepped out of the shadows, pulling a rolling suitcase behind her. Malice shimmered in her eyes.

"What's going on here? I thought you were dead." I took a step backwards. Jenny walked around me and locked the door with a little smirk.

"Lots of people did. That was kind of the point."

Ryker peeled a big string off his cheese stick, chuckling to himself. "People are so stupid. They'll believe anything if there's enough smoke and mirrors around it. You figured it out, though. I guess that makes you slightly less dumb than the average idiot. But then you came here by yourself so... you're stupid again."

"You can't kill me." I swallowed. "My friends know where I am."

"There's no way anyone would have let you come here alone on your wedding day, in your wedding dress." Ryker peeled off another bite of string cheese, keeping one eye on me. "Sorry."

Jenny removed a gun from the back of her jeans and

pointed it at me. My whole body tightened. "You can't do this! The Gherkins! Mike's parents! They're gonna... They're gonna..." My shoulders slumped as I remembered. The Gherkins spent every Christmas and New Year's in the Bahamas.

Jenny cackled. "We can do whatever we want up here. It's up to you how the rest of this plays out." She nodded to Ryker. "Tie her up."

"Wait!" I stumbled back. He paused. "If you kill me, someone's going to connect the dots. It may not happen right away, but they'll discover my body, and they'll figure out who did it. But you don't need to kill me because I'm not here to take you to jail."

They exchanged a curious look. Jenny's shooting arm did not waver. She kept a finger on the trigger.

"I'm here because I want to make a deal," I said. "Whatever you make on that painting, I want a third of it."

"Not a chance," said Ryker.

"I deserve it," I said. "Mike left me at the altar. He... He owes me this."

"Oh, my goodness." Ryker tossed back his head, rolling his eyes. "If I hear one more person talk like getting left at the altar by my gross cousin is such a big deal, I'm going to lose it! Do you not recognize that love is a fallacy? By chosing him you were abandoning yourself! My cousin, may he rest in peace, did you a favor by leaving you up there!"

"We're not cutting you in," said Jenny.

"Give me ten percent." I wasn't sure what I was doing. But I needed to buy time, and my negotiation strategy was the best one I had. "You have a kid. You deserve more than me. Five percent! Five percent and you'll never hear from me again."

"You're lying," Jenny said. "You'll be coming back to us,

asking for more money, holding this over our heads forever."

A sudden realization occurred to me. "Ryker, when you mentioned Mike just now you said 'rest in peace.'"

"Yeah. So?"

"Mike was brutally bashed in the head. Whoever did that doesn't care if he ever finds peace. But you meant it when you said that. You didn't kill Mike." Ryker started to reply, but I talked over him. "I bet you've known about the missing Rembrandt for years. You had a feeling Mike might have taken it, but you couldn't prove anything. Then he turned up dead and you connected the dots. Whoever killed him must have taken the painting, then you stole it directly from the killer." I turned to Jenny, speaking and moving with more confidence now. "But how did you get involved?"

"This is all wrong." Jenny's gun hand started shaking slightly. "We are killers. And we'll kill you if you don't back up!"

I took a step toward Jenny. "You're a mother, not a murderer. Once I figured out you'd stolen the painting, you knew the cops wouldn't be far behind. That's why you faked your own death. It was the only way for you to make it out of town with the painting in your possession."

"We killed Mike. And we took the painting. And we'll kill you too." Ryker puffed out his chest. His bravado belied his fear. "Shoot her, Jenny."

I scrubbed my hand over my face. What were Mike and Priscilla arguing about at the Christmas tree farm that day? They had just announced their future wedding to the world. But that fight... It came right at the beginning of all the chaos...

I gasped. "The pre-nup."

"What are you—" Ryker began.

"After Mike proposed to me, he forced me to sign a pre-nup. Wouldn't tell a single soul about our engagement until I signed it, actually. And he and Priscilla had just announced their engagement the day before he died. She signed it, but she really, really didn't want to. It's hard to feel loved when someone's lording a pre-nup over your head. I know that better than most."

Ryker struggled to find words. He looked over at Jenny but she kept her eyes focused on me.

"Priscilla was so upset about the pre-nup that *she* stole the painting from Mike, thinking that if they ever split up, she'd sell it in order to get her share of the money." I continued. "He found out. They got in a fight. She lost control. Bashed him over the head. You two pieced it together. You told Priscilla you'd keep her secret if she'd give you the painting, so she did. But she's a fighter. There's no way she's going to let you get away with that art."

"She doesn't have a choice, and neither do you." Jenny took a deep breath.

"Wait." My mouth went dry and my eyes widened. "Where's Priscilla?"

Jenny stepped toward me, finger on the trigger. Then...

Bang. Bang. Bang.

She hit the ground in a pool of blood.

47

ALL DRESSED UP AND NO ONE
TO KILL

*P*riscilla stepped into the room through a cloud of smoke. Ryker, who had knelt beside Jenny, stormed at her with a primal scream. Priscilla stood her ground, backhanding him with the butt of the gun when he got close. Her face was expressionless as his head hit the stairs and he went motionless.

The entirety of the case flashed before my eyes as I charged toward Priscilla. Mike dead on the ground. The safe left open and empty. Priscilla arriving home moments after the dead body had been found.

I saw myself alone on the altar, waiting for Mike to show up. I remembered my time alone in Jersey City. The day Miss May visited me there. I remembered the day I met Wayne.

She must have rushed back after kick boxing and killed Mike, I thought. *That means everything she said about the therapist was a lie. That means—*

Bang!

Priscilla fired in my direction. I fell out of the way just in time to hear the bullet splinter the banister behind me.

Bang! Bang!

Bullets made holes in the wall behind me. I lunged toward Priscilla and elbowed her across the face. When she turned back to me, she smiled through a bloodied mouth.

"Nice dress."

I was not in the mood for witty banter. Justice needed to be restored. Mike deserved it, Pine Grove deserved it. I deserved it.

Priscilla caught my next punch and used it to toss me into the wall behind her. I spun back before she had a chance to descend on me, landing a knee in her stomach. In a swift motion, I pulled off a wedding heel and brought it down on the back of Priscilla's hand. She screamed and dropped the gun, which skittered toward the front door.

When she turned back to me, Priscilla's look of placid menace transformed into an enraged scowl. She grabbed me by the shoulders, spun me around and tossed me into the wall. Yanking at the train of my wedding dress, she pulled me to the ground. I landed with a crunch and felt a sharp pain shoot up to my shoulder.

There was so much adrenaline coursing through me, the pain barely lasted more than a second. I scrambled to my feet, clutching my injured shoulder. Priscilla approached me with a predatory stride, a twisted smile playing on her lips. The room seemed to close in around us, the air thick with body heat and anger.

Summoning all my remaining strength, and all the karate Master Skinner had taught me, I launched a powerful punch at her face. She dodged and weaved with fluid grace, apparently summoning the kick boxing skills Master Skinner had taught *her*. It was as if Priscilla expected my every move and was always, somehow, one step ahead of me.

With each punch, the pain in my shoulder worsened. Eventually, Priscilla overcame me with her relentless fury, nailing my torso with one shot after another. I was tired, hurt, and wearing a wedding dress. The fight was hers to lose.

Priscilla landed a bone crushing kick to my abdomen. I doubled over in pain, gasping for breath, fighting with all I had just to remain standing. The room spun around me. My body felt heavy, as if the weight of all that had ever happened to me – with my parents, with Mike, and back in Pine Grove – was pushing down on my shoulders.

Priscilla circled me with sadistic pleasure dancing in her eyes. She knew she could finish me just as she'd finished Mike. My eyes darted toward the gun near the front door. It was too far. A flicker of doubt crossed my mind.

Was I strong enough to win this fight? If I wasn't, what would happen to the people I love? How would Wayne ever move on? How had I been so arrogant as to pursue the killer all by myself?

But then a surge of determination blasted through my veins. I refused to give up. I refused to let Priscilla get away with what she'd done. Pushing through the pain, I called on my last ounce of energy and launched a desperate attack.

My fists connected with Priscilla's jaw, sending her stumbling backward. For a fleeting moment, I thought I'd won the fight. But she swiftly regained her balance, eyes burning with a cavernous ferocity.

With a calculated strike, she delivered a powerful kick to the side of my head, sending me crashing to the floor. The room spun into a blur as darkness crept over my consciousness. As I lay there, I could hear Priscilla's mocking laughter echoing through the room. She loomed over me with a triumphant sneer. She was holding the gun.

Despite the odds, despite the pain, I refused to accept defeat. I clung to a whisper of hope. I closed my eyes. I prayed.

"Police! On the ground!"

Bang. Bang. Bang.

I opened my eyes. Priscilla lay beside me on the floor, clutching a bleeding arm. Chief Sunshine Flanagan rushed toward her, pulling handcuffs off her belt.

"Hey, Chelsea. Big day. Congrats." She grinned as she cuffed Priscilla and dragged her to her feet.

"How did you..."

"No time to talk. You're late for a very, very important date. Merry Christmas, by the way."

48

SOMETHING BORROWED, SOMETHING BLUE, NO BLOOD STAINS

*N*o. I didn't get any blood stains on my wedding dress. Yes. I triple-checked on the way to the church, just to be sure.

When I first got there, I thought I might have been in the wrong place. The entrance to the old stone church was empty. Garland, wrapped around the banister leading to the door, blew in the wind. There might as well have been tumbleweed blowing across the parking lot. That's what the vibe was.

But I'd called Miss May on my way over. Fine. Technically I'd *returned* the dozen missed calls I'd registered from her while I was over at the Gherkin's. I knew I was at the correct church.

Small. Quaint. A far cry from the brutalist, modern church Mike had insisted on years prior. This building was a perfect representation of what I wanted from my life moving forward.

Strong. Simple. Packed with family and friends.

The big, wooden doors groaned as I pushed them open. Over a hundred pairs of eyes turned and looked at me. In an instant, I took in the faces of so many close friends and townspeople, along with the gorgeous holiday decorations in the church. Wayne rushed down the aisle, past a row of poinsettias, hurrying toward me from the pulpit. and the crowd broke out into hushed, excited chatter.

"Chelsea!"

"Sorry I'm late. Um. I tried calling you." Christmas lights twinkled on a tree up front. Rows of garland were strung on every pew. "This place looks incredible."

"Miss May told me what was going on. But still. I was freaking out for a minute there!"

Someone called out from the crowd, "We all were!" A chorus of agreement followed as others chimed in. I took a step back and addressed them.

"Hi everyone. I'm here. I'm happy to see you all. And thank you for your patience!"

Everyone laughed. Miss May edged her way down a long pew and made a straight line toward me. She wrapped me up in a huge hug, right there in the middle of the aisle.

"You're OK!"

"We just talked five minutes ago," I said.

"But now you're here. I can see you, I can feel you. You're alright." Miss May turned to the crowd. "She's alright, every-one! And she caught another killer."

The townspeople cheered, hooted, and hollered. My face reddened as Teeny approached with her arms spread wide. The hug she gave me is quite possibly the firmest and most aggressive hug I'd ever received in my entire life. "Can't believe you did all the exciting stuff without us."

"I didn't do it all by myself," I said.

"What is that supposed to—"

A priest took his place at the pulpit. He tapped on the

microphone. "Hello everyone. Chelsea. Glad you've joined us."

"Happy to be here, Father," I said.

"Shall we get this show on the road?"

Humphrey piped up from an aisle seat a few pews in. "Let's do it already, William. I'm hungry for my Christmas dinner."

Kayla the wedding planner shuffled everyone into their places, directing Wayne back toward his groomsmen, and yanking me back toward the entrance to the church. Suddenly, Tom Gigley was playing "Hark the Herald Angels Sing" on the huge church organ, and just like that, I was headed toward my future as Mrs. Wayne Hudson.

Several years had passed since my near-miss wedding to Michael Gherkin, of the Blue Mountain Gherkins. Now I was getting married again, heart still racing from my battle with Mike's killer, which, poetically, had been his new fiancée, and somehow, the whole thing felt less stressful than it had the first time around.

I suppose, when you're marrying the person you're meant to be with, that has a way of slowing life down for a moment. What more could you ask from the person you love, anyway? The slower life goes, the more we get of it. I, for one, want to live as fully and as long as I can.

Father William (a balding priest of around 60) began by welcoming everyone to what he called the strangest Christmas mass over which he'd ever presided. Wayne and I had worked with him a bit, so he knew our story, and he recited it back in a little speech he gave about the two of us.

At one point, Father William said to Wayne, "Now, I know Chelsea catches all the killers in Pine Grove while you don't do much at all. But you can't expect things to keep up that way in the home, Wayne. You're going to have to chip in!"

That got a huge laugh, especially from Wayne. Then the priest said something about how married life is no *mystery* and people laughed even more. As the laughter rolled around the gorgeous room, I scanned the audience for Sunshine Flanagan. I'd insisted that she come to the wedding after she saved my life back at Priscilla's, but she hadn't shown up.

Probably booking Priscilla down at the station, I thought. *Now focus on the handsome beef, I mean man, in front of you*!

"Do you, Chelsea Rae Thomas, take Wayne Francis Hudson, to be your husband?"

"I do."

"Do you, Wayne Francis Hudson—"

"I do, I do!"

Teeny jumped to her feet. "Let's get to the kissing!"

Father William laughed. "In the name of the Holy Spirit, I solemnly declare you husband and wife. Let no one put asunder those that have been joined together today in the presence of almighty God. You may now kiss the bride."

We kissed. Everyone in town stood and cheered. They applauded for what felt like forever. We pulled apart. I looked out over everyone I knew.

Rita D'Avola wiped her eyes with baby Vinny's shirt sleeve. Sudeer and his wife stood hand in hand, beaming out the biggest smiles I'd ever seen from either of them. Miss May and John Wentworth smiled with poise and dignity. Patrick Ewing watched from nearby. Humphrey was asleep in a back pew. Liz, the local reporter, was taking pictures and notes from nearby. My cousin Maggie and my new BFF Aidy flanked my side of the aisle. KP had his arms crossed and was trying to look tough, but I swear I saw a tear on his cheek. My Aunt Deedee had her eyes closed and her hands in prayer position. Emily, from the ice cream shop, was beaming. Granny, Teeny's mom and the namesake of *Grandma's*, was doing a crossword. Brian from the *Brown Cow* was clapping. And Big Dan handed a sobbing Teeny tissue after tissue after tissue.

When it was time to leave the church, I shot a look over at Tom Gigley and smiled. "Hit it, Tom!" Without missing a beat, he leapt into the jazziest version of "Jingle Bells" I'd ever heard. The entire church burst out in song, including me and Wayne, and we danced back down the aisle, husband and wife.

EPILOGUE

$\mathcal{T}$he Thomas/Hudson wedding was a legendary affair in the town of Pine Grove. At my insistence, the theme of the party was 'you do you!' That meant that guests could wear tuxedos if they wanted. Or they could wear their pajamas. Or they could wear pajamas that looked like tuxedos.

I wanted to be my wedding to be the kind of place people felt comfortable being themselves. There were no big rules to follow, nor was there any invisible etiquette of which everyone needed to be aware. There was just a whole lot of fun, a whole lot of dancing, and a whole lot of incredible food.

Wayne and I really wanted to keep things casual and fun, so we decided on a "Breakfast for Dinner" menu that was silly and carefree. Once she got over the fact that I wouldn't let her cater, Teeny even mentioned how delicious everything was.

My favorite passed appetizer was the "Eggo Taco", which was eggs and cheese wrapped in half an Eggo waffle, drizzled with a little sour cream and hot sauce. Other appetizers included homemade mini-muffins (chocolate, blueberry or Cinnamon Toast Crunch flavored), something called 'bacon boats', which KP loved, and fresh fruit arranged like tiny Christmas trees.

The Christmas trees! How could I have forgotten to tell you about the Christmas trees?

Wayne held me back a beat before we entered the party. We were outside the event barn, and it was a chilly Christmas night, so I wanted to get inside, but he insisted.

"We need to talk about something important."

"OK," I said. "But make it quick, 'cuz our adoring public awaits us just behind those doors."

He grinned. "Remember how we lost the florist, and I couldn't find any new flowers, and Kayla couldn't either?"

"We don't need flowers if we have each other."

"I agree. Totally. That's very romantic. But I was talking to Miss May and KP a little while back, and we came up with a little solution..."

"And that is?"

"Follow me."

Wayne took my hand. Hercules opened the event barn doors and we stepped inside. The partiers cheered for us as we entered the room. I waved and Wayne and I danced in time with a festive song played by *The Giggles*. But it was only a few seconds before I saw Wayne's gorgeous solution to our flower problem.

Dozens of Christmas trees lined the room, each one twinkling with strands of twinkling lights, and decorated with homemade ornaments. I danced over to the closest Christmas tree. It was a bit lop-sided, with a patchy hole near the top. I laughed.

I spotted KP nearby and gave him a huge hug. "The ugly Christmas trees! People bought them for us!?"

"Guess so," said KP. "You look beautiful, kid."

Wayne smiled so wide that the energy from it jumped from his face to mine. He plucked a little ornament from the tree. "And each ornament has a little message from someone in town."

I took the ornament from Wayne. The message read:

"CONGRATS ON FINALLY MARRYING THE BEEF BOY! <3 TEENY"

I wanted to read every ornament on the tree, but the band was playing "Celebrate Good Times, Come on!" My feet couldn't resist. I dragged Wayne out onto the dance floor. The people of Pine Grove followed behind us in droves. Every minute of the wedding felt like it had been plucked from my dreams... Until the end.

Sunshine Flanagan slipped into the back door of the barn like a cat burglar. I had about half a slice of wedding cake in my mouth when she and I made eye contact. Sticking to the edge of the room, she floated toward me with downturned eyes.

I finally swallowed my bite of cake as she closed the distance between us. I greeted her with a sheepish grin. "You caught me in the middle of my second slice of cake."

"Hi, Chelsea. Congratulations. You look amazing."

Flanagan hugged me, almost without giving it a second thought. The hug surprised me so much that I actually said aloud, "Oh. We're hugging. OK. We're hugging now."

She ignored the awkward narration and, as we separated, kept hold of me by the shoulders. "I'm leaving Pine Grove. But I didn't want to go without congratulating you in person. Send my best to Wayne, too."

Flanagan looked over her shoulder, then back at me. She was wearing loose-fitting cargo pants, a flannel shirt and a baseball cap. It was almost as though she was in disguise.

"What's going on?" I said.

"Remember how I told you about my ex?"

"Hard to forget women who also have a murdered ex. And that was pretty recently."

"There's been a new murder in my hometown. Word is, the killer left the same signature at the scene of the crime." Her eyes got steely and determined. "I'm going back home, Chelsea. This killer is going to strike again. But next time, I'm going to be there. I'm going to catch them before they have a chance."

Suddenly, I had Flanagan wrapped up in a tighter hug than the one she'd used when she greeted me. And I was once again narrating. "I'm hugging you. We're hugging now."

"I can feel that."

Flanagan's green eyes were deep and searching. I saw in her a tenderness and vulnerability I'd never noticed before. But it made sense that she'd been hurting all along. Hurt people can be hostile or rude or downright mean. We've all been there at one time or another. I know I have.

"You're going to be Chief of Police somewhere new?"

Flanagan shook her head. "If there's one thing Pine Grove has taught me, it's that amateur sleuths are far more effective than the police. I'm following in your footsteps." She gestured around the room, still twinkling under the light of a hundred Christmas trees. "Coming back home has worked out for you, hasn't it?"

"It certainly has." I smiled. "Good luck, Chief."

"Please. Call me Sunshine."

The End

AUTHOR'S NOTE

Dear Reader,

Out of all the Apple Orchard Mysteries, this one was the hardest to write. I think that's because there's a bit of a finality to the story here.

When we met Chelsea, she was at a church, trying to get married. We all know how that worked out (RIP, Mike). In this story, she finds herself back at the altar. She *almost* misses the wedding. But she makes it to the church on time, and we get to see her finally say "I do" (and to the right guy this time).

Life is filled with uncertainty. Back in Book One, I'm not sure Chelsea grasped or accepted that. She wasn't healed from losing her parents. She was fighting to make sense of a world in which the only logic, often, is that there is no logic.

When we accept that fact — when we surrender to the uncertainty while still holding trust in our hearts — that's when good things happen.

I'm not sure what's next for Chelsea, Teeny, and Miss May. Most likely, I'm going to take a moment to reflect on these 20 books before jumping into Book 21.

In the meantime, I'm off to the races on the Sunshine Flanagan Mystery Adventures.

Sunshine, like Chelsea, has been on quite the journey in this series. At times, she's been downright nasty to our heroes.

But she's been fighting a battle none of us knew anything about.

Life can be like that, can't it?

Do you want to see Sunshine Flanagan redeem herself? Do you want to get to know who she really is inside?

Do you want her to catch the killer who murdered her boyfriend, and finally get the validation and support that she deserves?

CLICK HERE TO READ THE EXCITING PREQUEL TO THE SUNSHINE FLANAGAN MYSTERIES – "MURDER ON THE BRIDGE"

Thank you all for sticking with me through these books. Here's hoping for a lot more where they came from.

Warmly and with love,

Chelsea

Made in United States
Troutdale, OR
08/15/2023

12091481R00130